BIGGER

BIGGER

★ ★ ★

PATRICIA CALVERT

Atheneum Books for Young Readers

B-1 9/95 PQ 10.50 Book Fair '94

Atheneum Books for Young Readers
An imprint of Simon & Schuster Children's Publishing Division
1230 Avenue of the Americas
New York, New York 10020

10 9 8 7 6 5 4 3 2
Printed in the United States of America

Library of Congress Cataloging-in-Publication Data
Calvert, Patricia.
Bigger / by Patricia Calvert. — 1st ed.
p.   cm.
Summary: When his father disappears near the Mexican border
at the end of the Civil War, twelve-year-old Tyler decides to go
after him and bring him home, acquiring on the journey a
strange dog which he names Bigger.
ISBN 0-684-19685-9
[1. Frontier and pioneer life—Fiction.
2. Fathers and sons—Fiction. 3. Dogs— Fiction.]   I. Title.
PZ7.C139Bi   1994   [Fic]—dc20   93-14415

With affection—to two who once upon a time
shared a dormitory room with me in North Hall
at the University of Montana—

★ ★ ★

Camille Olson Gregory
and
Ruth Trzcinski Schott

★ ★ ★

BEFORE . . .

On July 4, 1865, four months after the end of the Civil War, several hundred men gathered along the banks of the Rio Grande near Eagle Pass, Texas. These men, led by General Joseph O. Shelby, commander of the Iron Cavalry Brigade from Missouri, had never surrendered to the Union forces. They vowed they never would.

One of the soldiers held the Stars and Bars aloft, the symbol of Confederate dreams. After he had lowered it and spread it on the ground, General Shelby threw down the black plume he'd worn in his hatband throughout the war. The flag was wrapped around a stone. Then stone, flag, and plume were pitched into the muddy waters of the Rio Grande, where they sank out of sight as a lone bugle sounded taps.

It had taken the troops twenty-nine days to cross the Texas plains; now they planned to raft across the river and escape into Mexico. There, with the help of Emperor Maximilian, they hoped to rearm themselves, to eventually retrace their steps across the border, and restore the Confederacy to the glory they believed it deserved.

1

The day was hot; the men were tired. Many wore tattered Confederate uniforms; others were dressed in threadbare civilian clothing. Yet the spirits of these men were high; they were bound together by a deep conviction regarding the principles of the four-year conflict they'd fought and lost.

Now they were prepared to leave behind parents, wives, children . . . farms, homesteads, businesses . . . to cast off old defeats and take up a new dream. The quest they shared was an irresistible magnet that drew them across the wide, brown river that flowed below. . . .

☆ 1 ☆

TYLER LIFTED A PALE GREEN BEAN TENDRIL AND COAXED it around the wooden arm of the trellis. There. He'd finished all four rows of pole beans. He straightened, and rubbed the hollow of his back. It was sore; tonight he'd have to sleep on his side, his knees tucked up, to give himself a little ease.

Tomorrow, though, he'd tackle the potatoes that still needed hilling. Then the whole garden would have been tended to—peas, beans, potatoes, squash, turnips. The corn in the field behind the house, high on the slope where it got plenty of sun, was already six inches tall. It would be a good year for crops, the best in the four long years since Papa rode away.

The boy shaded his eyes, squinting against the evening sun, glad the day was almost over. He could see that Mama had already lit the lamp in the kitchen. He hoped she was making biscuits for supper. He'd eat several, slathering each with gleaming brown ribbons of sorghum. The cow had come fresh a week ago; Mama and Rosa

Lee had churned this morning so there'd even be butter on the table tonight.

Tyler turned when he heard the sound of a horse crossing the narrow bridge over Sweet Creek. It was rare that anyone traveled up or down the road anymore. When Papa was home, of course, visitors came as regularly as bees making their rounds; folks for miles in each direction had craved the company of Black Jack Bohannon.

The boy looked hard at the rider. Suddenly he couldn't breathe. His heart refused to beat. Then he sucked the warm evening air deep into his lungs. *The moment was unfolding exactly as he'd dreamed it would.* A month ago, on Palm Sunday, April 9, 1865, General Lee had surrendered to Ulysses S. Grant at Appomattox over in Virginia, and the long war had ended. And now—now, at last— Papa was home.

Tyler watched as the rider came slowly up the lane, his heart swollen and tender with happiness. A moment later, though, a vague unease settled on him.

Papa certainly hadn't ridden away like that, had he? Shoulders hunched, chin resting on his chest as if he were in prayer? No. He'd gone off high-headed and proud, his big red horse as eager to be off to war as he was himself. Doubt kept the boy from running to the fence and calling Papa's name as he'd done in all his dreams: "Papa! Oh, Papa, we've waited so long!"

But Tyler knew the war had done awful things to people. Maybe to Papa, too. Why, hadn't it killed Oat Snepp's brother, and many others all through these soft Missouri hills, no matter whether they fought on the side of the Union, like Billy Snepp, or with the men in gray, like Papa?

4

Oat's family got a letter, bordered in black, from Mr. Lincoln. Oat carried it to school, then hung, red-eyed, on to a tree in the school yard while Mr. Blackburn read it aloud to everyone.

Tyler could still hear the schoolmaster's voice, solemn on the morning air, while Oat hugged the tree as if he believed sooner or later it would hug him back. Oat's brother had fallen at Stones River; it was a name that had a pleasing sound. As Mr. Blackburn read, Tyler imagined a place where clear water ran over smooth black and gray boulders, and found it hard to believe that's where Billy Snepp did his dying.

Tyler walked to the fence. The top rail was level with his breastbone, and he pressed against it hard to keep his heart quiet. The rider came closer; finally, he lifted his head out of the lavender shadow cast by his hat brim.

Tyler stared. His heart returned to its familiar, shriveled size.

The stranger's beard was as thin and pale as corn silk, not as thick and dark as a beaver's pelt. His eyes were as gray as his uniform, not as black as a gypsy's, and there were blue puddles of weariness beneath them. When he finally spoke his voice was as light and soft as air. Papa's had been as rich and thick as molasses.

"Evening, son."

"Evening," Tyler replied, then added cautiously, "sir."

"You live close by?" the stranger wanted to know. There was a deadness in his voice that made Tyler think of ashes in a cold grate on a chilly winter morning.

"Up there," Tyler said, dropping his own voice to a whisper. He pointed up the hill toward the house, whose

5

kitchen window now glowed cheerfully in the falling blue dark of May.

"Reckon your mama and daddy could spare a tired traveler a meal and a bed for the night?" the man asked. He did not refer to himself as a soldier, Tyler noticed.

"Might be they could," Tyler answered. He decided it would be best not to mention that Papa hadn't come home from the war yet himself.

"Maybe you could ask them for me," the stranger suggested.

"Yessir," Tyler agreed, stepping away from the fence, "I'll surely do that."

"I'll wait here," the stranger offered, crossing his hands on the scarred pommel of his saddle. "I don't want to cause a fuss for anyone in case there's no food or any room to spare," he murmured. "For all of us, this war has been . . ."

The soldier hesitated, and seemed to search his mind for the right words to describe what the ordeal had been like. "It has been hard on everyone, North and South, blue and gray, black and white. It left many of us—ah!— so much different than we ever thought we'd be," he concluded, so softly Tyler could barely hear him.

Tyler nodded, as if he understood how that could be. None of Papa's letters made the war sound quite like the stranger just did, though.

"I'll come right back," he promised. "Papa—my father—he got back a week ago, and went to fetch a bull calf from a farm over yonder. He'll likely be late getting home for supper tonight." It was a lie, of course, but Tyler decided maybe it was a necessary one.

He studied the stranger a moment longer. "Papa being

6

late and all, might be my mama could let you have his portion," he offered, elaborating on the fib just a bit.

Tyler glanced back once as he ran up the hill. The stranger waited in the road, head lowered again onto his breastbone, his horse with its eyes closed, too, as if they were once more offering evening prayers. In the darkness the blooming dogwood on the opposite side of the road looked like mist rising off the creek.

The man wasn't Papa, which after four long years was a terrible disappointment. But his uniform was gray, which meant he might have ridden with General Shelby's Iron Cavalry Brigade, too. And maybe, after several warm biscuits and sorghum, after Mama had poured him a second cup of strong, black coffee, the stranger might have news to share. He might even be able to tell them what had happened to Papa.

"Because I have to know," Tyler declared softly as he stepped onto the porch. He reached for the latch on the kitchen door. "Even if it's like Mama always says, that Papa most likely is dead, that we'd have heard something from him by now if he wasn't, I still have to know." If your father was Black Jack Bohannon, a man who fit his name like few other men fit theirs, and if you were his oldest son, you couldn't let yourself rest easy until you'd found out what his fate had been.

MAMA, HER CHEEKS PINK WITH EXCITEMENT, WAS NOT HER steady self at all as she set an extra cup and a plate on the table.

The stranger sat in Papa's chair under the window (no one had used it since Papa rode away), and Rosa Lee and Lucas sat to his left, their black eyes wide and surprised in the smoky yellow light of the kerosene lamp. Maggie lay on the hearth, her new pups still so small they looked like fat brown sausages fastened to the teats on her belly.

Tyler imagined the stranger, being hungry, perhaps having gone days without food as he hurried home from the war, would eat like a wolf—or at least like a man who hadn't had a good meal in a while. Instead, he accepted a single biscuit almost reluctantly, buttered it, sweetened it with only one thin ribbon of sorghum, then ate it as discreetly as a lady at a church social.

Tyler cleared his throat. As the man of the house, he felt obliged to make conversation. It was something Papa had no trouble doing at all, and if he'd been home he'd

8

have filled the room with questions and comments in his strong, dark, gypsy voice.

"Where do you hail from?" Tyler began. Papa might have been bolder, but to the boy it seemed like a safe beginning.

The stranger chewed slowly. "A ways from here, son. Near where the Wyaconda River runs into the Mississippi." Tyler hoped the stranger would go on but he continued to chew in his picky way. Tyler decided to frame his next remark so it wouldn't sound as if he were prying, yet would encourage the guest to be more forthcoming.

"Papa—John Bohannon is his name but folks in these parts have always called him Black Jack—rode with General Joseph O. Shelby. I was wondering if you might have heard—"

"Ah, Jo Shelby," the stranger echoed. His smile barely lifted the corners of his mouth but he nodded as if the name were familiar. "I didn't ride with that brigade myself but I saw him once. Not a big man as men go; went about with a long black plume stuck in the headband of his hat. They claim he had twenty-nine horses shot out from under him, yet was never harmed. 'If my mount's a red one, I know I'll never be killed in battle,' he claimed. Yep, an unusual man in more ways than one."

It was Tyler's turn to nod. Papa's horse, Ransom, was a fine, blood-colored bay; did that mean he'd never get killed in battle either? "In more ways than one?" Tyler pressed eagerly. He needed to know more about this man, Jo Shelby, of whom Papa wrote so often in his letters.

"Among other things, he's never surrendered to the Union," the stranger answered. Across the table, Lucas's

9

and Rosa Lee's eyes were as round as saucers, and their biscuits cooled on their plates.

"But the war's over now," Tyler put in, "so I suppose Jo Shelby will have to give up just like everyone else."

The stranger raised his pale brows. "I heard the general's running like a fox. Unless those Federals are as fleet as hounds there'll be no defeat for *him*," he murmured, his smile neither joyful nor bitter.

Mama seemed surprised. "And why not, pray tell? Like my boy Tyler just said, sir, the war is over. With God's grace everyone can go back to living regular lives again. Surely you don't exclude General Shelby!" Her voice was heated, and Tyler knew exactly what worried her heart: If Jo Shelby was on the run, Papa might go following after him.

"Those are easy words, ma'am. But some men don't give up their dreams as easy as others."

Tyler fidgeted. Hadn't he planned to eat at least three or four biscuits tonight, to smother them in butter and sorghum? Why, yes, but something much more important had stolen his hunger away.

"Won't they hunt him till they catch him? General Shelby, I mean?" Tyler asked, and laid his fork beside his plate as he waited for the stranger to drain his coffee cup.

"I heard he was leaving the country," the man murmured. "That he'd rather quit the South itself than ever give up to a Yankee. For some men, the idea of the Confederacy went bone deep, you see. The fact that General Lee surrendered to General Grant at Appomattox Court House over there in Virginia never cut it with the likes of Jo Shelby."

"Leaving the country?" Tyler repeated. But why would

10

a man leave the country? Lincoln had kept it together, hadn't he, and one way or the other didn't everyone have to haul in the same harness, pull in the same direction now? Isn't that what the Union victory meant?

"He's going over the border, son," the stranger explained. "Far and away, beyond the reach of the long arm of the government up in Washington."

Over the border? What border? Tyler tried to imagine where this border might be that the stranger spoke of. Perhaps the stranger meant General Shelby was headed out west, where it was said a man could get land for free, that all he needed to do was prove it up by homesteading it. The West was so wide open that states still called themselves territories out there because they hadn't been admitted to the Union yet.

Or maybe the stranger meant way up north, to that place called Canada. On Mr. Blackburn's map at school it was colored green, and looked even bigger than the United States. If that's what Papa aimed to do, he'd surely have let his own family know, wouldn't he?

"They're going down to Mexico," the stranger went on, and allowed Mama to pour him another cup of coffee. Her hand trembled, Tyler noticed, and he sensed the dread she felt. Then it was just as the boy hoped: After more coffee, with another warm biscuit in his belly, the stranger seemed almost eager to share everything he'd heard.

"General Shelby's drummed up a ragtag mix to go with him—about six hundred men, I hear—and hopes he'll pick up more volunteers along the way," he said. "He aims to cross the Rio Grande at the Texas border, then talk Emperor Maximilian into giving him a hand with his schemes. Once in Mexico, you know, the Union men can't touch a hair on those boys' heads. Then, when he gets up enough militia, Shelby intends to come back and wage war against the Union all over again."

Mexico. So far from the soft hills of Missouri!

Tyler knew almost nothing about Texas, even less about Mexico. He imagined the sun must shine down there all the time, that there'd be no hills, no meadows, no clear, clean streams as there were in Missouri. Why would a person want to go to such a place when they could come back here, to a snug cabin on Sweet Creek, to a wife and three children, a cow who'd just come fresh, a garden that was already half-grown? Most of all, to a son who'd been waiting four long years? . . . But in his heart Tyler knew if Papa was still alive, if he still had two good legs, could load his rifle quick as ever, then he'd surely be on his way to Mexico with General Shelby.

The stranger spread the blanket Mama had given to him on the clean straw in the empty stall next to Calico. Her week-old calf, as sweetly spotted as its mother, poked its wet, pink nose through the slats as if it, too, wanted to hear what was going to be said.

"No need for you to stay up with me, son," the stranger murmured kindly. "From the looks of that garden, you've put in a long day yourself, and you must be as tired as me. I'll just stretch out here, and be mighty grateful for the hospitality."

Tyler lingered. "What you said about those troops headed for Mexico," he began slowly. "Any chance they'll change their minds?"

Before settling back the stranger sat a moment with his

arms looped around his bent knees. "Oh, no doubt a few will give it up. They'll get to thinking about home, you know, about the life they're throwing over. But others . . ." He narrowed his eyes in the soft glare of the kerosene lamp that Tyler held.

"Son, there are some chaps who cleave to a notion like others cleave to a piece of ground or to their children and womenfolk. Me . . ." He stopped, and smiled apologetically.

"Well, I'm a man who only wants to go back to that place I came from, up where the Wyaconda runs into the Mississippi, where my kin have lived since before the century turned. I did what I figured was my duty—but back home, why, I've got me a boy about your age! A good boy, and I want to see him again quick as I can. My wife, too, and all those good places to hunt and fish that I thought for sure I'd never see again when dead men lay all around me and bullets whined past my ears thicker'n swarms of hornets."

The stranger stopped, and the boy realized he'd said about all he had to say. Yet there was something Tyler still needed to know. "How far do you figure it is?" he asked, dreaming a dream even though he was standing upright, eyes wide open, not even sleepy yet.

"How far is what?"

"Mexico. How far is it from Missouri, do you s'pose?"

"Oh, a mighty long way, son. Must be nearly eight hundred miles as the crow flies, probably a whole lot farther on foot."

Tyler hesitated a moment. "How would a person get there—if he took a mind to, I mean?"

"Well, I guess you'd—here, wait a minute. I have

13

something that might . . ." The stranger got to his feet, reached into his pocket, and drew out a tattered, grayed piece of paper. "I got this here scrap of a map," he said, "that might show you what you want to know." With a stub of a pencil he wrote something on the back, then held it out.

When Tyler touched the paper something happened inside him. Until that moment he hadn't been sure exactly what the dream in his head was all about; its outlines were fuzzy and faint. Clutching the piece of folded paper, they suddenly came into sharp focus.

"Thank you kindly," Tyler murmured. "I'll see you in the morning. Should I leave the lamp with you?"

"No, son, carry it back to your mama. Thank her for the fine biscuits, and give my regards to your papa when he gets home tonight."

Halfway back to the house Tyler stopped and blew out the lamp. Overhead the stars looked closer and friendlier than they had in a long time. He paused in the path, held the lamp against his chest where the chimney glass warmed his breastbone, and thought about what he'd just heard.

Eight hundred miles as the crow flies, the stranger had said, a lot longer on foot. Yes, Tyler agreed silently, that was a long, long way. Was it too far to go to live the dream that was now fully shaped in his head and heart?

★ 3 ★

IN THE MORNING TYLER HURRIED DOWN TO THE SHED TO milk the cow, then turn her and her calf out to pasture. The stall next to Calico's was deserted. A hollow in the straw showed where the stranger had slept; nearby, Mama's blanket was neatly folded.

"Is he coming up to breakfast?" Lucas wanted to know as soon as Tyler got back to the house.

"I want that man to talk to us some more," Rosa Lee whined, her words blurry with sleep.

"He must've got up and left early," Tyler told them. "I don't think he wanted to take any more charity from us than he needed to." Lucas was disappointed, so Tyler added, "He told me he had children of his own at home, that he'd been away from them a long while. He was eager to get back to 'em soon as he could."

"Papa will want to get back to us right quick, too," Lucas predicted, his voice holding no doubt about the truth of what he'd said. "It will be nice when it's all like it used to be," he added, smiling a private smile.

Rosa Lee frowned, and dug at her eyes with her fists.

15

"But I can't 'zactly rec-amember how it used to be," she complained. "I can't even rec-amember what Papa looks like!"

"You can't remember," Tyler corrected.

"That's what I said!" Rosa Lee said crankily, stamping her bare foot. "I tol' you, I can't *rec-amember!*"

"That's because you were so little when he left," Mama soothed. "No more than a baby, barely a year old, not even walking good yet."

Tyler left the three of them to their chattering and quickly ate a cold biscuit with a little butter and a crunchy sliver of honey and comb laid on top. This morning he'd get after the potatoes he hadn't tended to yesterday. He'd check them for bugs, too; if he found any he'd tell Lucas how to take care of them. The day would be a long one so he'd best get started quickly. Then, if he finished early enough, he and Lucas could go fishing one last time.

By midafternoon the potatoes were all done. From the looks of the crop, there'd be at least ten bushels to take in come September. In the cool root cellar Papa had built into the hillside behind the house, they'd keep fine until next year, along with the turnips, both put down in moist sand to keep them fresh and crisp.

Tyler dug some worms, put them in one of Papa's old tobacco tins, then looked around for Lucas. "Lucas, how about you and me going down the creek to fish for a while?" he called to his brother, who was playing near the swing that dangled from the oak tree in the yard. Lucas hurried to get the poles, and in a moment they were walking downstream to where the creek was clearest and deepest.

16

"Mama will be glad to have fish for supper," Lucas announced, pulling his first shiny, brown trout out of the water. Tyler watched his brother carefully as they fished together first on one side, then on the other side of Sweet Creek.

In lots of ways, he was relieved to see, Lucas wasn't just a little kid anymore. Not like Rosa Lee, who still was. Why, from the looks of Lucas, maybe he'd be as tall as Papa someday. His hair, like Rosa Lee's, was already as black as Jack Bohannon's, his eyes almost as dark.

It worried Tyler a little that he himself didn't seem to be growing very fast anymore. He didn't relish the thought of growing up to look like Uncle Matthew, Mama's brother, who was short and square and ordinary, who had hair the same plain, dull brown color as a muskrat, not glossy and brown-black like a beaver's. His own eyes were the same common color as Mama's, not as sly as a gypsy's. Well, no matter; the fact that Lucas was no longer a little boy would make what was going to happen tomorrow a lot easier.

By the time the sun dropped behind the blooming dogwood along the creek, Tyler was pleased to see that between them he and Lucas had caught a mess of fourteen fish. Plenty for supper, enough so that maybe he could take two or three with him in the morning.

After supper—Mama fried the fish in bacon grease, and baked a batch of cornbread, too—Tyler checked on Calico and her calf. Lucky the calf was not a little bull; it meant that in a year or two, when she was old enough, she, too, could be bred and they'd have two milk cows then, with milk enough to sell for extra money.

Tyler checked on the chickens. Three of the hens were

17

nesting clutches of twelve or thirteen smooth brown eggs. If Maggie could leave her mothering long enough to keep the skunks and possums away, there'd be plenty of fryers for Mama to butcher in the fall and put down in glass jars for the winter.

Tyler took a swing through the corn, inspected the garden one last time, adjusted the latch on the fence, and, noticing it was loose, wished he had time to fix it before he left. Even so, when be brought Papa home, Black Jack Bohannon would have no cause to say, "Why, what've you been doing, boy, laying on your backside the whole time I was off to war? Place looks a mess!" No indeed.

In the morning Tyler rose quickly, even before he heard Mama stirring. Across the room Rosa Lee sucked her thumb with a steady, rhythmic slurp, and Lucas lay flat on his back, his mouth open, sleeping deeply. Before he could think about it twice, Tyler bent swiftly to place a kiss, light as a moth's wing, on his brother's left eyebrow. He couldn't have done so if Lucas had been awake. It would have flustered them both.

Tyler didn't smooth the quilt over his bed but stretched it flat, laid a pair of trousers on top, then added an extra pair of socks and shoes, and lastly his worn jacket. He rolled it all up tightly and tied it with rope he'd carried up from the cow shed.

From the tin box he kept under his bed Tyler took the pale, blue-white aggie that Papa had brought home as a gift from Uncle Matthew's store. "It's a lucky piece, Ty," he'd said with a wink. "All of us need as much of that as we can get!" He took three of Papa's letters out of the box, letters that had been read so often their edges were soft and gray, their ink beginning to fade. He included the stranger's map, checking first to read what had been written on the back. Only two words: *Good luck.*

In the kitchen he wrapped two of the fish from last night's supper in some paper, added four biscuits left over from the night the stranger had eaten with them, then stuffed everything into the end of his bedroll. Maggie stood close by, her red tongue lolling out of her mouth. Tyler smoothed her sleek, speckled-hound head with his palm, and poured her a bowl of milk.

"You take care a those chickens, hear?" he whispered, and she wagged her whole back end as if she understood. "Your pups too." He knew he didn't have to tell her how to be a good mother, though. Maggie was the best mother to her pups any hound could be, and his only regret was that none of the four of them, not even the husky male who'd been born first, was old enough to be taken along for company.

He made a fire in the grate of the cold stove, set water on to wash with, and waited for Mama to get up. When she did she seemed startled to see him up and dressed, his eyes not cloudy and full of sleep as they usually were.

"What's this?" she asked, a smile making her blue eyes as light as a summer sky. "Up already, water heating so soon? Does Mr. Blackburn have plans for all of you this fine Saturday morning?"

Tyler shook his head. It was going to be hard to say what he had to say. There was no other way than just to tell his plan straight out. "No, Mama. The thing is, Mama, I'm going away."

"Going away?" Mama put her hand over her heart, and Tyler knew that she already knew, that she'd known what he would do even as the stranger had talked at the table two nights ago about General Shelby heading for the Rio Grande.

"To Mexico, Mama," Tyler told her. "I'm going off to find Papa. I know I can. And I know he'll want to come home, too, if I can just tell him how much we need him."

"You don't know any such thing," Mama objected. "Your papa was very keen on the Confederacy, remember. He volunteered long before anyone else in this whole valley did. If General Shelby leaves the country, your papa will go with him." Her face was suddenly pale, and Tyler figured he knew what was going through her mind: *One of my men left me and never came back; now another one is going to follow him.*

"Anyway, I 'spect your Papa is probably dead, since no one's heard a word from him in more than a year," Mama insisted, as if she needed to say something truly shocking to make him come to his senses.

"Why, that stranger from Indiana was on *his* way home, and your papa would be here by now, too, if something terrible hadn't happened to him. I don't really believe he's with General Shelby, son, about to run off to some foreign land. He's dead and gone, most likely, and we'll never see him again in this world."

Tyler caressed the edge of the table. It was as worn and smooth as marble beneath his fingers. *Ah.* Marble was used for gravestones. He stoutly refused to let himself think about that. Papa was alive; he could feel it in his bones.

"It might be that Papa's wounded," Tyler countered. He didn't really want to quarrel with Mama, but it was

20

important that she understand what was in his heart. "Might be he's lost a leg and can't travel fast. Maybe he got blinded. Remember, Harold Crowe said in church one day that men lost pieces and parts of themselves like leaves falling off the trees. Said he was lucky to have lost only an eye. That's what he said, Mama. You heard him, same as me."

"So," Mama said with a sigh, "you really mean it then." She wrapped her hands in her apron as if they were suddenly chilled and needed to be warmed.

"Yes, Mama, I really mean it," Tyler whispered, then added, "but I'll be home right quick. I won't waste time searching in places I don't think Papa could be. By the time you and Lucas are ready to take in the potatoes in September, why, I'll be here to help you. Papa too."

Mama moved away, her eyes glistening, and Tyler watched as she spooned some honey into a small jar. "Take this with you," she said, in a toneless voice that made it plain she realized nothing she could say would change his mind. "Here are some apples, too, ones I'd been saving to make dumplings with."

Lucas clumped flatfooted into the kitchen, prying his eyes open with his fingers. "Where you goin', Ty? Hold on, I'll come with you!"

"Not this time, Lucas," Tyler replied. "I'm going to find Papa and bring him home." Rosa Lee, following behind Lucas, her red, swollen thumb still stuck in her mouth, started to whimper. "B-b-but if you go away like P-P-Papa did . . ."

"Lucas here will look after things while I'm gone," Tyler told her, and noticed that Lucas drew himself up taller to hear him say so. "Yessir, Ty, I'll do my best," Lucas whispered, and Tyler knew his brother was eager but scared, too, at taking on the job.

"You'll do fine," he assured Lucas. "And something else, Lucas. You tell Mr. Blackburn I'll be missing the last three weeks of school but that I'll be back again come fall." Lucas nodded, pale and proud to discover he'd also be the carrier of important messages.

"I don't know which way you plan to travel," Mama said when they stood on the porch, "but it'd be a good idea to make your first stop at Uncle Matt's place. Might be he could help you get outfitted a little better than you are. You'll need matches and suchlike but I don't have enough to spare you any." Uncle Matthew still ran his store down in New Hope. He hadn't gone to war because he'd lost most of a leg in a sawmill accident when he was only a boy.

Tyler nodded; it was what he'd already decided to do. He stepped off the porch and went through the gate where only two nights ago he'd welcomed the stranger. He noticed again that the latch needed tightening, and called over his shoulder. "Lucas, this here latch needs some fixin'. See to it if you get the time, hear?"

Behind him, he knew the three of them stood hip to hip on the porch, watching him hike off down the road, would stand there until he'd vanished into the thin May air. Part of him wanted to turn around, to wave, even to run back and say he'd changed his mind. The other part, the part that was about to do something a grown man might do, wouldn't let him.

There was no way he could expect to get all the way to the Rio Grande, Tyler realized, if he kept looking over his shoulder at Mama twisting her hands in her apron, at Lucas standing taller than usual, at Rosa Lee, whose cheeks would be stained the color of strawberries by her crying.

The journey before him would be a long one. He'd need all the courage he could muster to get all the way to Mexico by himself, to find Papa, to bring him back. And if he found only a grave with a crude wooden marker along the way? Then he'd lay his hand on his heart, Tyler vowed, and would say a prayer, but at least he'd know what Black Jack Bohannon's fate had been.

Tyler squared his shoulders. He didn't look back.

★ 4 ★

TYLER TOOK NOTE OF THE FAMILIAR SIGHTS HE PASSED, storing each one in his mind to be taken out later, like a tintype, when he was far from home.

In the early morning light he saw a doe and her spotted fawn fade noiselessly into the underbrush as he passed by. Grapevines covering the rail fence were in bloom; Mama would be able to make jam in the fall. At the top of the hill there were three wild apple trees, their white blossoms making him think of three sisters in pale dresses on their way to church. Good pictures to carry along to remind him of where he'd come from.

On the bridge that crossed Sweet Creek, Tyler glanced into the dark water below, hardly rippled at all this particular morning, and caught sight of his own reflection. His image down there was meek and insignificant. He glanced away quickly. No, that wasn't a picture he'd save. He couldn't carry anything with him that would make him feel as if he might not be able to do what he'd set himself to do.

He walked steadily until noontime, his old, soft hat clamped low over his eyes. By then the sun had warmed the back of his neck until it felt tender to touch, and his belly growled with hunger.

On Easter Sundays long ago, when Papa had hitched Ransom to the wagon and taken them all to Uncle Matthew's, the miles had dropped away right smartly. Perhaps having company had made the time go faster. Back then Lucas had been a little tad, Rosa Lee not even born yet. On foot, though—and all by himself—the miles seemed to creep by at a turtle's pace.

At the fork in the road—one way went to New Hope, where Uncle Matt lived, and the other turned west, toward McMinnville—Tyler passed a tree that cast an umbrella of shade on the ground. He walked gratefully into that cool darkness, and sat a while before he plucked a biscuit and some honey out of his bedroll.

He'd hardly eaten a bite two nights ago when the stranger was at the table; now he could easily have eaten a dozen biscuits, even ones as dry and hard as these had gotten. He nibbled at one of the fish, eating everything slowly to make it last longer.

When he finished he washed his hands in the creek, and, making a cup of his palms, drank deeply. He was tempted to lie down in the shade, to rest a little longer. No, he couldn't do that, but perhaps he could spare a moment to read a few lines from one of Papa's letters. Tyler fished in his pocket, opened the letter, limp from being folded and refolded so often, then began to read aloud to himself.

"Dear Family—

Now don't I wish you could meet this General Shelby! He's thin as a whip, and don't seem much taller than son Ty but he's hard as flint. Size don't make a man a hero; it's his heart that accounts for that, and this chap's got one the size of a mountain lion. I'm mighty proud to ride off to war with him. We'll give those Union boys a shellacking for sure!"

Size don't make a man a hero; it's his heart that accounts for that. Tyler folded the letter, feeling braver already. Papa said it didn't matter if a person was thin and small (he himself was only twelve to boot) if he had a big heart.

It would be a good thing to read a few lines from Papa's letters every day, Tyler decided, most especially when he needed courage. But now it was time to get back on his feet, back out there under the warm Missouri sun. He couldn't afford to let himself backslide, to go easy on himself even before he'd truly gotten started on his journey.

Tyler whistled from time to time, but that seemed to take too much energy, so he walked in silence. Bit by bit the countryside became less familiar. In the distance he now and then saw a small farm. A dog, far off, barked occasionally. On porches he could see folks shade their eyes to study him as he passed down the road.

He calculated how long it would take him to get to Uncle Matt's store in New Hope. Once, Papa told him that a man could walk at the rate of one mile every fifteen minutes if he walked along at a good pace. In an hour, then, a person ought to be able to cover four miles. If you divided thirty by four you came up with about seven and a half hours to New Hope.

But Tyler realized he wasn't walking quite that fast. Besides, he had to rest every now and then—not too often, of course—which meant, all in all, it could take him as long as ten hours to get to Uncle Matt's. With luck, though, he'd get there by suppertime. Tyler's mouth watered as he thought of the table Aunt Margaret always set.

He thought of Uncle Matt, too. Folks said—too often, in Tyler's opinion—"Now ain't you a boy that takes after his Uncle Matt!" He'd never told anyone so, but he prayed he'd *never* be like Uncle Matt, who was so, well, dull. There was no blaze about the man; the fire inside him burned low or maybe had never burned at all. That long-ago accident at the mill must've made him overly careful and cautious. If a boy had his choice, wouldn't he want to be like Black Jack Bohannon? Of course he would.

Until Papa went away they'd gone to Uncle Matt's house in New Hope every spring; but the sight of the white front of Riley's Farm and Home Store had never looked as welcome to Tyler as when he spotted it through the screen of hawthorn trees that bordered the road.

It was dark enough that lamplight already showed in all the houses in New Hope; it was plainly past suppertime. Aunt Margaret would warm something up for him, though. Having had only one child—Cousin Clayton—she always made a fuss over him and Lucas and Rosa Lee whenever they came to visit.

Ah. Cousin Clayton.

In spite of his weariness Tyler gritted his teeth. Somehow it was hard to warm up to Cousin Clayton, even

27

though they were almost the same age. Clayton had a tendency to . . . the only word was *whine*. Seemed like he was a boy determined to stay younger than he really was, to be his mama's darling brown-eyed baby boy forever. Clayton had never been the oldest, Tyler reflected, since he was the only one. He'd never been responsible for milking a cow, planting a garden, putting vegetables down in a root cellar, or butchering chickens.

Tyler hesitated a moment outside his uncle's store. Truth to tell, Uncle Matt had hair the color of a muskrat's hide, was short and sturdy and sensible, not a man people would give a lively nickname like Black Jack to, but it had to be admitted he was mighty successful.

Tyler didn't like to think about it too often, but he'd heard stories about how unhappy Mama's family had been when she ran off with "that gypsy fellow." Papa wasn't a gypsy, of course, not like gypsies in far-off countries. It was only that he was a little larger than life, a man whose voice was richer, whose hair was blacker, whose teeth were whiter, a man who liked a horse with plenty of spirit, who sometimes came home from town smelling sweetly of whiskey. But he was—why, he was Papa: He was Black Jack Bohannon. He couldn't be measured by the same yardstick that was used for other men.

In addition to the handsome front Tyler had seen from a quarter of a mile away, Riley's Farm and Home Store had a porch with carved railings that spanned the whole face of the building, providing townsfolk with lots of places to sit after they'd done their shopping. Out behind were several outbuildings because Uncle Matt kept a livery stable too.

A CLOSED sign was hung in the front door of the store, so Tyler took himself around to the back. As he came up the right side of the building he saw a dog tied to a stake, halfway between the house and the livery barn. It strained forward on its chain and gave him a low, warning growl. The hair on its dark neck stood straight up, its lips were peeled back to show red gums and gleaming white teeth. There was something odd about the dog, something peculiar about the way it looked at a person, not to mention its menacing growl, so Tyler turned away. He thrashed through a lilac hedge, and came up to the back door from the opposite side of the store.

On the back side of the building, where Uncle Matt had his living quarters, there were lace curtains on the windows. Through them Tyler could see his uncle, spectacles perched on his nose and a newspaper on his knee. Aunt Margaret sat nearby with her crochet work. Clayton was nowhere to be seen. Tyler tapped lightly at the door, hoping his cousin had already gone to bed.

There was a stir inside, and Tyler knew his knock had aroused a flurry of excitement. After all, it was dark, and there was a sign in front that plainly said CLOSED.

"Who? . . ." Uncle Matt asked as he opened the door to peer out. Then he exclaimed, "Why, Tyler!" A moment later his uncle's voice was filled with worry. "Boy, what brings you down here all alone at such an hour? Has something happened to your mama or—"

Tyler allowed himself to be pulled into the warm room, so well lighted and still fragrant with smells of fried chicken. "There's no trouble at home," he told his uncle quickly. "Mama sends her best to everyone, and Lucas

29

and Rosa Lee are fine." Clayton appeared from some-where and stood behind his mama, clinging to her as if he were no older than Rosa Lee.

Uncle Matt peered out the back door a second time before closing it. "I didn't hear that dog bark. How'd you manage to get past him? He came close to taking some-body's leg off a day or two ago."

"I came up on the far side," Tyler admitted. "He looked—sort of mean, not like our Maggie back home."

"Not like your Maggie is the truth," Uncle Matthew agreed. "That dog is the devil's own son, let me tell you, and nothing to fool with. Not to mention the fact I think he put my prize bluetick hound in the family way. What with him being so wicked and making pups with Daisy, I'm goin' to tell Henry to take him out in the woods and shoot him. I want to get shut of him for keeps." Then Uncle Matt turned his attention back to Tyler, a worried frown on his wide, pale face. "But if everyone at home is fine, what brings you way down—"

"I'm off to look for Papa," Tyler said. Just as with Mama, it would be best to spit the words right out. "A stranger who came by Sweet Creek the other night told us—well, now that the war's over I just have to go look-ing." He decided not to mention anything about going as far away as the Rio Grande or the foreign land of Mexico.

"Ah, yes," Uncle Matt nodded. "But it seems unlikely that you'll be able to find one lone man in this whole wide country. Might be a better idea if you just waited for your papa to come home under his own steam."

"The stranger who stopped—we never found out his name—gave me an idea of where to look," Tyler said, thinking it would be prudent to let Uncle Matt know he wasn't exactly going off to look for a needle in a haystack.

Aunt Margaret smoothed his hair with a disapproving cluck, then went to the stove to warm up some supper for him. Still clucking like a hen, she set him a place, and filled his plate with a mountain of snowy potatoes and three pieces of crisp, golden chicken. Seeing the plate she set down, Cousin Clayton exclaimed loudly, "I'm hungry too, Mama!"

"Why, Clayton, you ate enough to feed an army not an hour ago," Aunt Margaret reminded him with a fond smile.

"But I want to eat again!" Clayton yelped, eyeing Tyler's plate as if it were a special treat he hadn't been invited to share. When his mother fixed him a plate, too, Clayton sat across the table and shoveled food into his face as if he hadn't been fed in a week. No wonder all his edges were round and smooth, Tyler decided, rather than sharp and lean, as would be more suitable on a boy his age.

"There's plenty of space for you to sleep in Clayton's new room," Aunt Margaret said.

Clayton groaned. "Can't you put Cousin Ty somewhere else, Mama?" he asked.

"Shush, Claytie, and mind your manners," his mother cautioned with a wag of her finger. "I'll get out a straw pallet and put down some quilts, Tyler," she went on, "and we'll fix you up snug as a bug in a rug."

Clayton glowered from across the table, even though Tyler pitched friendly glances his way. If a person was an

31

only child, Tyler reflected, he most likely didn't want to share even a minute of his mama's and daddy's attention. He got so used to being the main attraction that he probably believed he was as rare as a two-headed calf in a circus. The thought of Clayton, the One-of-a-Kind Boy locked in a cage, going from town to town with a circus, made Tyler smile.

"What you grinnin' about, mister?" Clayton demanded as he licked a chicken bone as clean as a whistle, his small brown eyes squinty and mean.

"Nothing," Tyler murmured, trying to wipe the smile off his face. "I was just thinking someday I'd like to see me a circus."

Upstairs, after Aunt Margaret made him a tidy pallet on the floor across from Clayton's cot, Tyler got ready for bed. Cousin Clayton was still crabby. "Crazy as a cootie bug, that's what you are!" He snorted, softly enough that his mother wouldn't hear as she went down the stairs.

"You're as big a fool as your papa. I heard *my* papa say he was! My papa said going to war was just an excuse for Black Jack Bohannon to go off adventuring," he went on. "He wouldn't have been conscripted, him having a wife and three children and being a farmer to boot. Never was much of a farmer, though," Clayton finished with a superior sniff.

"You button your lip about my papa," Tyler warned, "or I'll button it for you." He rose off his pallet, and threatened Clayton with a raised fist.

"You lay a hand on me and I'll yell for my mama!" Clayton bleated, hunkering down in his covers.

"Sure you would!" Tyler hissed. It felt queer to be fighting with someone. Days and weeks went by when

32

he and Lucas never said a cross word to one another. Maybe Clayton was an only child because he was such a pain in the neck his folks decided to quit after they had just one.

In a fit Clayton blew out the lamp. "Too bad if you're scared of sleeping in a strange place in the dark," he said as if he hoped Tyler would begin to whimper. Tyler listened to his cousin thrash about in his bedclothes, and was relieved when Clayton finally settled down.

I'm already thirty miles from home, he thought with amazement, pushing Clayton's words out of his mind. Thirty miles, which hardly amounted to a hill of beans considering how far he had to go, yet here he was at Uncle Matt's, a good meal in his belly, sleeping in a clean bed. It was probably the last clean bed he'd see until he stopped back this way many weeks from now with Papa in tow.

Blocks of moonlight were scattered across the floor of Clayton's bedroom, and suddenly Tyler thought of the dog he'd seen tied in Uncle Matt's yard. Listening carefully to make sure Clayton was truly asleep, Tyler got up from his pallet and crept to the window.

In the yard below he could see the dog Uncle Matt called the devil's own son lying in a silver ribbon of moonlight stretched between the house and the livery stable.

Maggie used to love moonlight, too, Tyler remembered. She'd turn her sleek, speckled-hound head up as if it were a cavalry bugle, would play herself such a fine tune that Papa had to fetch her indoors to sleep by the fire for fear she'd rouse folks miles away.

Below, the devil dog made no sound. He lay fixed and

silent in the moonlight. Waiting. Watching. For what? Tyler wondered. The May air felt suddenly cool, and the boy shivered, then crept back to his pallet. He tugged Aunt Margaret's quilt up to his chin. If it was true, as Uncle Matt had warned, that the dog belonged to the devil, it would be wise to have nothing whatever to do with him.

★5★

TYLER MET UNCLE MATT DOWNSTAIRS EARLY, BEFORE ANY-
one else was out of bed. His uncle beckoned him through
the door that separated the family living quarters from
the store.

"It won't do to send you off without a few supplies,"
Uncle Matt said, picking a slim, metal container from a
shelf. "This will help to keep your matches dry," he
explained, and filled it with as many matches as it would
hold.

Then he selected several tins of meat from another
shelf and got a can opener from a drawer. "These will
only do you for a few meals, Tyler, then you'll have to
think of something else," he warned. "Might be you'll
have to do a little mooching as you travel along." Next he
selected a handsome knife with a bone handle from a
glass case, then a small whetstone with which to keep it
sharpened. Finally he picked out a large blue kerchief.

"I noticed the back of your neck was burned near to
blistering," he murmured. "Going farther south this time

35

of year the sun will only be more unforgiving. Wear this, it will keep you comfortable."

At breakfast Aunt Margaret was much noisier about his leave-taking than Mama had been only yesterday. Why, it was almost as if for a moment she believed she *was* his mama! If she had been, Tyler thought, her carrying on would've made it twice as hard to take up the second day of his journey. He was glad Mama was stony faced and brave, her pain showing only in her eyes, not her words.

"Your daddy's probably lying in his grave as we speak," Aunt Margaret wailed loudly, her voice colored by the same whiny note as Clayton's. "Landsakes, you're only a boy, never been out of these hills before. No telling what might become of you!"

When her back was turned, Clayton got in a few licks of his own. "All I can say is you must be daft, Ty Bohannon!" he hissed. "Going off to look for somebody who's dead or don't want to be found, otherwise he'd a come home by now like most everyone else!" But when Tyler looked Clayton square in the eye—in the morning light Clayton's eyes were a dim, yellow-brown that matched his muskrat-colored hair—he understood what was really eating at the other boy.

Why, if I invited him to come along with me, he'd join up quicker'n a cottontail, no matter how hard his mama cried and begged him to stay home! Tyler realized. The thing that was bothering Clayton, it was plain to see, was envy. Even if Aunt Margaret had hollered after him, "No, no, Clayton, don't leave your dear mother, my darling baby boy!" Clayton would have gladly run upstairs, made himself a bedroll of his own blankets, and hiked off down the road without a backward glance.

36

Tyler knew there was no way he could issue any such invitation to Clayton, though. On this journey he'd have to travel light and fast. Unfortunately Clayton was on the chubby side, not a light, lean, fast kind of boy at all.

Anyhow, Clayton would be gone from home only a day or two before he'd begin to complain about sleeping on the ground and not having regular food and would want to go back to his mama after all. Worse, he'd insist he couldn't find his way home alone. It would mean hiking back with him over many miles, a waste of precious time. No, there was no way Clayton could be invited to go along, even though the prospect of having company all the way to Mexico tempted Tyler mightily.

"Now is there anything you want me to do while you're gone, son?" Uncle Matt asked in his serious, sensible way when they walked out to the road after breakfast.

"You could make a trip up to Sweet Creek or send a letter to my mama and Lucas and Rosa Lee," Tyler suggested. "Tell them I got this far, let them know everything's all right with me, and make sure everything's all right with them."

"Yessir, I'll do that; you can rest easy on it," Uncle Matt agreed. He shifted his weight off his wooden leg and reached into his pocket. "I want to give you some money, Tyler. You'll need it, and I know you're not a boy to waste much, not like that papa of yours sometimes did."

Tyler wished he hadn't said that about Papa, but he accepted the coins and the paper money that Uncle Matt laid in his palm. At this Clayton's eyes got narrow, turned from yellow-brown to pea green, and his lips sewed themselves into a nasty little knot.

37

"Papa, I reckon I need some money, too!" Clayton squawked.

"No such thing, son," Uncle Matt said, his words firm but not crabby. Then he limped beside Tyler to the edge of the road, while Aunt Margaret waited on the porch and held on to Clayton. As he and Uncle Matthew passed the barn, Tyler spied the devil dog in an L of shade cast by the corner of the building.

Tyler tried not to look at the dog but somehow his glance was drawn irresistibly toward the animal. The expression in the creature's eyes chilled him to the bone. It was as if the dog intended to cast an evil spell on him. Tyler's heart went still in his chest. What if there was no way to ward off such a devil curse and it turned his long journey into a disaster?

Although it was a gloomy thought to recall Uncle Matt's words—that the animal must be shot—perhaps it'd be best, Tyler decided. After all, if the devil really was hiding inside him . . .

Then, after a second uneasy glance, Tyler understood why the dog's gaze was so compelling: Its eyes were of two different colors.

One eye was brown and warm, like an ordinary dog's, but the other was as cool and blue as a bit of milk left at the bottom of a tin pail. Suddenly, Tyler thought of the blue-white aggie buried in his pocket. Yes, it was that same bleak, faded color all right. Out of that pale eye seemed to stare an altogether different dog than the one that looked out of the brown eye.

"I see you're wondering about that critter's eye," Uncle Matt remarked. "It's not a blind one, as some folks make the mistake of thinking," he explained. "Why, he'll bite you just as quick if you come up on his blue side as on his brown side."

"Looks like a glass eye to me," Tyler murmured, fingering the aggie in his pocket and remembering the feeble, pale-eyed old horse Mr. Blackburn rode to school. He cut himself a wide path around the dog.

"There was a strange fellow who came through New Hope a few months back," Uncle Matt went on. "Nobody knew who he was, where he came from, or what his business was. Nobody trusted him far as they could pitch him, though. Disappeared one day as quick as he showed up but left that dog behind, tied to a fence over there," he explained, pointing down the street. "I've always figured he was descended from one of those sheepdogs from Scotland, them having different-colored eyes as they sometimes do. Long as I've had him chained up he's been looking down that road. Wondering, I s'pose, if that chap will ever come back to claim him."

Then they were at the road themselves; there was no more time for talk about dogs abandoned by their masters. It was time to say farewell. Uncle Matthew held out his hand. "I wish you Godspeed and good luck, Tyler," he said. There was something wise and gentle in his voice, as if he understood this was a journey that had to be made, even though he himself was a sensible man who'd never do what the son of a man with a gypsy heart had to do. Favoring the Union as Uncle Matt did, he'd never have chased after Jo Shelby anyway, even if he'd had two good legs.

Tyler felt his uncle's warm hand on his shoulder. "And if you find your papa, you stop here again on your way home and stay the night with us, hear?" Tyler was grate-

39

ful Uncle Matt seemed to bear no hard feelings about Papa's choice in the war.

"Thank you, sir," Tyler said. "And I'll take care of the money and bring back what's left over."

Uncle Matt smiled. "If you spend it all, son, that's fine by me. That's what I meant it for."

"Say good-bye to Cousin Clayton for me," Tyler urged, then fibbed a little. "Tell him I'll look forward to seeing him again when Papa and I stop come September."

Uncle Matt, with a half salute, turned back to the pair who waited for him on the porch of Riley's Farm and Home Store. Tyler waved to Clayton, who kept his eyes fastened on the toes of his shoes and refused to wave back.

Just as when he'd left his home place, Tyler didn't treat himself to any backward glances. Yet he couldn't resist a final sideways peek toward the barn, and felt a cool finger of dread tickle the back of his neck when he realized the devil dog's gaze of blue and brown was following him. Tyler hustled out of view, grateful when the row of hawthorns cut him off from the sight of Uncle Matthew's barn and store.

At nightfall, in a thick grove of willows along a creek bank, Tyler decided to make his first camp. He'd been gone from home two days now, and reckoned he must have covered nearly sixty miles or more. But this night would be different because it would be the first one he'd spend all alone. Now the comfort of Clayton's bedroom— even with Clayton across the room snoring louder than an old man—seemed sweetly safe.

But aloneness is something I'd better get used to, Tyler

reminded himself, since he had more than seven hundred miles yet to travel. He gathered himself a few stones to make a ring in which to build a fire. Next he cut some branches with his new knife, and made himself a pallet of leafy willow twigs on which to spread his blankets.

By the time everything was done it was quite dark, and he decided to eat. Aunt Margaret had packed two big pieces of chicken for him that were twice as good as they'd been the night before. He gnawed every bit of flesh from the bones and pitched them aside, then drank water from the tin cup she'd packed for him. She'd even included a wedge of cake, crumbly now in its paper wrapper, but still delicious.

As the campfire burned down, the stars overhead loomed brighter, and the moon could be seen riding above the soft black crowns of the willows. Tyler crept to his leafy pallet and stretched himself out.

He'd never slept out alone before.

He'd never realized the woods were full of so many sounds.

Sounds such as a person never noticed when he was snug inside a cabin.

Ominous sounds. As if unknown creatures were creeping close to where he lay. As if, at any moment . . .

Tyler sat up.

What was that sound he just heard? Had the underbrush cracked ever so softly, as if some sort of beast were sneaking closer and closer, intending to finally leap out with a snarl and attack him? He shivered with a cold sweat as he remembered stories about bears and mountain cats that Papa used to tell.

With a branch, Tyler stirred the fire to life. He saw

nothing in the blackness. No pairs of eyes surrounded him like lanterns in the dark. He settled himself down again.

He wondered suddenly: Had Cousin Clayton decided to traipse after him? Why, that darn mama's boy! I'll send him packing in the morning, Tyler vowed. "I have to travel fast, Clayton," he'd explain as kindly as he could, "so you'd best get on home to your mama and daddy where you belong."

The sound came again.

It was light, tentative; it couldn't be Clayton, who was as light-footed as a cow about to drop a calf. Tyler bolted upright. This time he threw an extra stick onto the fire so that it blazed up brightly. He heard the sound once more; it came from the opposite side of the fire.

Something *was* coming closer, closer through the underbrush, a few careful steps at a time.

Tyler grasped the narrowest end of the branch so he'd be able to whack the creature with the stout, clubbed end. He bit his lip hard, cranked his arm back, got ready to come down hard and splatter the brains of whatever beast poked its head out of the brush.

The low branches of the bushes began to part. Tyler couldn't swallow. His fingers felt stiff. His palms were sweaty. His heart hammered loudly in his ears. The branches moved, rustled, separated.

There, staring at him across the fire out of one blue eye and one brown one, stood the devil dog.

"Git!" Tyler hissed, his blood running like cold spring water in his veins. Instead of moving, the dog crept near enough to snatch up the bones Tyler had pitched away. A dog could strangle mighty easy on chicken bones, Tyler

42

knew, and at home Maggie was never allowed to eat them. But maybe that's what this beast deserved. If the dog choked and expired right here before his eyes, well, it would be God's will.

But the dog had jaws like a wolf's; he pulverized the little pile of chicken bones, swallowed them down without so much as a hiccup. He advanced around the fire, his large head held low, his queer blue-brown gaze fixing Tyler with a hypnotic stare. He laid down three feet from the end of the boy's bed of branches.

Tyler studied the dog.

The dog studied Tyler.

"Git on outa here!" Tyler ordered in a loud voice. The dog didn't move. How had he managed to get loose? Tyler asked himself. There'd been a heavy leather collar around his neck that was hooked to a chain staked in the ground in Uncle Matt's yard. Had he somehow managed to pull his head back through that collar? It seemed unlikely, because as Tyler looked closely he saw the collar had been fastened so tightly it had begun to wear off the hair around the dog's neck.

The boy stirred; the dog raised its head. The growl that came up from deep inside the animal's chest was soft, threatening. Tyler debated: Should he bring his club down on the dog's head right now, hard as he could? Perhaps he could kill the creature with a single blow.

He imagined the dog's bleeding head, the dazed look that would come into its one blue and one brown eye. But what if the dog didn't die right off? He'd have to club it again and again. Lots of times, maybe, till his arm got so sore he couldn't deliver one more blow. The dog's skull might break apart, shatter like the leftover squash he and Lucas sometimes trashed on the rocks down by the creek.

The dog didn't move. Tyler didn't either. Finally he laid the stick on the ground beside him. He'd lie down himself but would keep the dog in plain sight, he decided. After a moment the animal closed its eyes, and Tyler was amazed at the difference: *It was only a dog.* A dog that made no sound, a dog that didn't remind a person much of a devil at all.

Nevertheless, Tyler vowed he'd keep his own eyes open all night long. Nossir, he wouldn't sleep a wink. When he woke in the morning, though, sunlight was splashed in brazen patterns across his bed of willows— and the dog was gone.

TYLER GOBBLED THREE BITES FROM ONE OF HIS TINS OF meat, ate a biscuit, licked up the leftover crumbs from the parcel Aunt Margaret had wrapped the cake in, then searched around his campsite for signs of the dog's footprints.

He couldn't find any.

Tyler frowned. The ground was dry, he observed, and covered with grass and leaves; under such conditions maybe it wasn't a surprise the animal hadn't left any clue that he'd shown up last night.

Or did I imagine the whole thing? Tyler asked himself. It gave him a spooked feeling to realize there was no way he could *prove* that a dog had lain across the fire from him last night, that he hadn't dreamed how the bushes parted, how he'd been transfixed in the gaze of those strange eyes, one brown, one blue. Then he remembered: He'd seen the dog snap up those chicken bones, wolf them down without even a belch. Well, then . . .

When he searched for the chicken bones there were none to be found anywhere, not even a scrap big enough for an ant to haul away. So it was true: He *had* seen what he thought he'd seen, hadn't dreamed a jot or tittle of it. Tyler couldn't decide if that discovery pleased or scared him.

Was it going to be the same ordeal each night when he made camp? That the animal would skulk around out there in the darkness, only to come creeping closer, closer as the fire died down? On a journey that was going to cover so many miles and last so many weeks such suspense would be awfully hard on a person's nerves.

Tyler got a drink of water from the creek, thinking as he did so how sweet a cup of Calico's warm, fresh milk would taste right now. Whoa! To recollect such small, homely details would be the same as looking over his shoulder, which he'd promised himself not to do either. He'd think only of the future, of knocking off thirty miles or so each day, of marking *X*'s off the back side of his map, above the spot where the stranger had scribbled *Good luck.*

He glanced around once, pushed dirt over the fire with the side of his shoe to make sure it was quelled, then loaded his pack on his back. He searched again, half superstitiously, for a pair of glowing eyes hidden far back in the bushes but saw nothing at all. It was time to go; his third day on the road was about to begin.

As he walked along Tyler felt peeved that Clayton's remark of yesterday morning still rankled him: *You must be daft . . . going off to look for somebody who's dead or don't want to be found.* But what did Clayton know? Clayton, who'd never done a bold thing in his whole life, who'd be his mama's darling brown-eyed baby boy till his hair turned gray! Of course Papa wanted to be found.

46

Halfway through the morning Tyler saw a cabin set far back from the road, one rather like his own on Sweet Creek. If it had been a fine, fancy house like some of the ones he'd seen in New Hope, he wouldn't have stopped, but since it was a familiar sort of place—common, a bit in need of repairs—he decided he'd take a chance.

Uncle Matt had warned that the tins of meat wouldn't last forever, that he'd have to figure out other ways to eat. He'd hinted mooching might be one solution. Begging didn't appeal much to Tyler, but if he offered to do chores for folks as he traveled along—hoe a garden, milk a cow, shovel out a chicken house—why, maybe he could earn himself a good home-cooked meal now and then.

When he knocked at the door of the little cabin, however, there was no answer. Then, from around the corner he heard the sound of someone chopping wood. He found an old woman there, doing up some kindling, while a few thin chickens pecked listlessly at the bare dirt around her feet. She jumped back when she glanced up to see him watching her, and laid a trembling hand across her breast.

"Don't mean to give you a scare, ma'am," Tyler apologized, "but when I knocked on your door and didn't get an answer I came around back."

The old woman sighed, and mopped her forehead with a corner of the ragged gray shawl that hung about her narrow shoulders. "This isn't my regular job but the old man has been down a long time. It was a matter of me doing it or it not getting done," she said, tucking a wisp of hair behind her ear.

"If you want an hour's worth of work I can pay you with a meal," she offered, holding out the ax, "but if it's

47

money you want you'll be out of luck. I got no money for you to steal, no mule, no horse either."

Tyler laid down his bundle and took the ax from her. "Sounds like a fair trade to me, ma'am," he agreed, pleased at how easily the deal had been made, and before she'd gotten to the back door he'd finished the chunk of pine she'd been struggling with.

Why had she thought he'd steal her money, mule, or horse? he wondered. Did three days gone from home make him look like some sort of criminal? He stacked all the cut wood neatly, like Papa had taught him, and when it seemed that he'd worked about an hour he went to the back door. He pointed to the woodstack.

"Does that look about right to you, ma'am?" he asked.

"Right enough," the old woman agreed, and let him pass through into her kitchen. "Son, you gave me a bad start a while ago," she told him. "Since the war ended folks say the country's being overrun by thieves. Scalawags is what they're calling 'em—and I was scared you mighta been one of 'em, come to rob me and my old man of what little we got left."

"No, ma'am, I'm not a scalawag and I don't aim to rob nobody," Tyler said. Although he hadn't meant to tell her about his journey that's exactly what he found himself doing over a bowl of chicken soup (which was so thin he decided the chicken had hardly got its feet wet as it ran through the broth). He told her how brave Jo Shelby was, how Papa had believed heart and soul in the war, that he'd probably decided to follow the general all the way to Mexico, not realizing how much he was missed and needed back home.

"Might be your papa is dead like so many others," the

48

old woman observed. Her voice was as dry and lifeless as corn husks in a November wind. So many people— Mama, Aunt Margaret, Cousin Clayton—said the same thing: Your papa might be dead, as if that was the only end they could imagine for him.

"I heard men were killed by the tens of hundreds in the war," she went on, "and were laid up in fields and along fences like cordwood. Even worse, when those boys were buried it wasn't each to his own grave, as any loving mother would pray, but their bodies were just covered over in a ditch like pigs that'd died of the plague."

Tyler doubted her words. It wasn't possible men would kill each other in such numbers, then stack up the bodies as if they were no different than the wood he'd just finished stacking outside. Most certainly they wouldn't be treated like dead pigs. People made up such tales because they didn't know any better. Why an old woman would make up such stories, however, Tyler couldn't explain to himself.

In a corner of the kitchen, the old man she'd spoken of slept on a narrow bed, his flesh yellowed and stretched like parchment over his skull, his mouth agape like a dark hole in his face, his eyes sunk deep in their sockets.

"He's waiting for the end," she explained simply. "He's had a long life, and when he's gone I don't aim to linger here myself. You see, our boys, Dolph and Joshua, both fell in the war. Now, the old man doesn't care if he lives or not and, truth to tell, my sentiments are the same." She sighed. "I say it's only fitting Lincoln himself went down."

"Lincoln himself?" Tyler echoed, puzzled.

"You didn't hear?" the woman asked, turning rheumy

eyes on him. "It was on a Friday, only a week after the war ended. Someone shot him. An actor, I heard, and he died the very next day."

Tyler remembered pictures he'd seen of Lincoln; Mr. Blackburn was fair-minded in class, and displayed photographs of both Mr. Lincoln and Jefferson Davis, the president of the Confederacy. A deep grief showed in both men's eyes, as if they regretted doing what they'd set their hearts and minds to do. But the stranger who'd stopped by Sweet Creek made no mention of Lincoln dying; either he didn't know himself or the old woman was being fanciful again.

Tyler was glad to find himself on the back stoop at last, in the sunshine, out of the house where death was happening and where he'd heard someone might have murdered the president. Before he turned to leave, the old woman handed him a jar with some leftover soup in it, a cloth tied over the top with a string. "Sorry I don't have a lid, son. You'll have to carry it upright till you eat it," she apologized.

Tyler told her he was pleased to have it, no matter how he had to carry it, and turned south when he reached the road again. It seemed unbelievable that a president could be killed like an ordinary mortal; such a man ought to be immune to the fate of regular folks. Lincoln dead? That man with somber gray eyes and tangled gray-black hair who'd kept the Union together in spite of men like Papa and Jo Shelby? Hard to believe.

As he walked, Tyler watched in the thick weeds of the ditches and farther back in the trees for any sign that the devil dog was following him. He saw nothing, only some scrawny cows in a distant field. Perhaps the dog had a plan of its own. Maybe it was seeking the master who'd left it behind. In that case, it wouldn't keep tracking *him* anymore. It was a thought that brought Tyler relief, and he walked along with a lighter heart.

When night came he once again searched for a snug campsite and finally found one in a grove of trees set like an island in the middle of a wide meadow of waist-high, wild timothy. He made himself a fresh bed of leaves and twigs, gathered dry, fallen branches for a fire, and settled himself down. Having already spent one night alone, he knew most of the nights to follow would be easier.

There was no way he could heat the soup in the glass jar the old woman had given him so he decided he'd have to eat it cold. No, wait. He could use Aunt Margaret's tin cup. Carefully, Tyler poured some of the soup into the cup, glad to see it contained a few pieces of meat (they were gray and tough; it must've been an old rooster that had ended up in the pot). He set the cup in the coals for several minutes, stirring the broth from time to time before he began to eat.

Then he heard the sound. Tyler stopped slurping.

Other than a cricket's chirp and the sound of an owl far away, he heard nothing more. He'd been mistaken, he decided. He began to eat again.

There came another muffled sound of footfalls through the meadow grass. This time Tyler knew it wasn't his imagination. He waited. The grass tops moved, but he couldn't see what made them tremble. They parted. Once again, there stood the devil dog.

"You," Tyler said flatly. On hearing a human voice, he reflected, an ordinary dog would react with a timid wag of its tail. This dog wagged nothing, didn't even lift an

51

ear. There was something so serious and steady in its eyes that Tyler couldn't tear his own glance away. The dog's brown eye studied him warmly, almost affectionately, while the blue eye regarded him with cool suspicion. The dog sat, its front feet placed precisely together, its head held high so its white chest faced the fire, looking as if a muslin bib had been tied around its neck. Tyler observed that the dog's ears were rather soft and down-tipped, like a shepherd dog's, but its muzzle was sharper, its forehead broader, like a wolf's might be, though his personal knowledge of wolves was limited to pictures he'd seen in one of Mr. Blackburn's books at school. Its coat was neither sleek like Maggie's nor shaggy like a collie's. Instead, it was dense, about two inches thick, such as a bear cub's might be. Except for its white bib, the dog was dark, not black exactly, more the charcoal color of a partially burned pine log.

"You," Tyler said again. "Come around for another handout, I expect," he accused. He continued to slurp the old woman's thin soup but left a third of it at the bottom of the cup, and held back two bites of biscuit. He dunked the biscuit in the soup and pushed the cup toward the dog. The dog backed away with a soft snarl. Tyler moved around to the other side of the fire so the dog would feel freer to come close.

The devil dog crept nearer, his belly low to the ground, until he reached the cup. In one quick gulp soup and biscuit vanished. The dog licked both sides of his mouth, eager to catch any dribble that remained, then sat back on his haunches again.

"Looks like you're an easy keeper," Tyler admitted with

a sigh. That's what Papa always said about Calico and Maggie. "Those gals are easy keepers, son, doesn't take much to make them happy," he'd say, with a wink in Mama's direction. Had he meant Mama was an easy keeper, too?

"But you're bigger than I figured you were," the boy observed. "Almost the size of a newborn calf." The dog's legs were shorter, of course, but lengthwise he seemed almost calf-sized. "Yes, bigger than I thought you'd be," Tyler mused.

Bigger.

"If you're going to show up for supper every night," Tyler told the dog, "you might as well have a name you can answer to." The dog seemed to listen carefully to his words.

"Can't call you Dog," Tyler pointed out. "That's no fit name. Can't call you Blackie because you're wearing that fancy white bib and aren't true black besides." He searched his mind. *You're bigger than I thought you'd be.* "What d'you think of Bigger?"

On the other side of the fire, the dog didn't say yes or no to the suggestion, but when Tyler lay down on his pallet he called across the dying coals.

"Bigger? You can stay here all night if you want to, Bigger." Maybe Uncle Matt was wrong; there didn't seem to be a devil inside the dog after all.

"It was God who gave you those queer eyes," Tyler reasoned aloud. "Doesn't have to mean there's something wicked about you, does it, Bigger?" He'd say the name often, he decided, until the dog got used to it.

The dog seemed to understand how things were going

to be now, and finally stretched himself full length beside the fire with a tired sigh. He closed his eyes as he'd done the night before, and after a time so did Tyler. When the boy woke in the morning, the dog was still there, wide awake, watching him expectantly.

☆ 7 ☆

TYLER FELT THE DOG'S EYES ON HIM AS HE REFRESHED the fire with a few twigs, spooned what was left of the old woman's soup into the tin cup, and set it to heat in the warm ashes. At the creek he scrubbed his hands and face, combed water through his hair with his fingers. All the while he knew the dog was hanging there on the bank, shy as a schoolboy new in class.

"Bigger," Tyler called, scooping up a drink of water for himself in the empty jar, "come on down and help yourself."

Slowly, his wide head lowered, his peculiar eyes seeming to divide him into one dog that was trustful and one that was skeptical, Bigger came closer. He stuck his nose in the stream, lapped up a quick drink, then looked about warily.

"Good dog," Tyler congratulated him. "See, that didn't hurt you a bit!" But when he reached out to stroke Bigger's head, the dog flinched. His upper lip curled back, showing rows of sharp, gleaming teeth. He laid his ears flat against his head, his powerful jaws snapped shut on empty air, and he backed off with a low, warning growl that came from deep inside his white chest.

"You might be an easy keeper all right," Tyler grumbled, snatching his hand away, his heart hammering, "but you sure ain't a quick one to make up!" For a fleeting moment he wished the dog could speak, that he could tell what had happened in the past that made him so scared of getting close, so afraid of even a kind word.

Maybe he'd been beaten, Tyler surmised; maybe he had good reason to be suspicious. After all, Uncle Matt had threatened to shoot him; well, maybe someone, somewhere had actually tried to blast him to kingdom come.

The only thing to do, Tyler decided, was give him room and in time—with luck—maybe he'd warm up. On the other hand, maybe Bigger was the sort of dog who'd never be a real pet. Maybe he'd never be a hearth-lizard like Maggie, toasting herself by the fire, first on one side, then on the other on cold winter nights as she thought it her right to do.

As Tyler had done the night before at supper, he ate his breakfast but left enough for the dog to have another serving of soup and part of the last biscuit. While Bigger snapped up his portion, the boy rolled up his pack, tied it, and smothered the fire.

The morning turned cool, and soon the sun was screened by a thin layer of clouds that took the glare off the landscape, making traveling easier. As he walked along, something began to nibble at Tyler's consciousness, and he tried to put his finger on exactly what it was.

Then it came to him: This would be his fourth day alone. He hadn't realized it would be so lonesome, going day after day with no one to talk to.

Back home, on a morning such as this, Mama would be making suggestions about the day that was borning. Lucas would be chattering like a magpie. Rosa Lee would be keeping up a steady stream of nonsense talk to the rag doll she'd dragged by the leg to the breakfast table. Even Maggie would be sighing and murmuring to her pups, and if he were there he'd have one or two things to say before he went out to do chores.

"I wonder if Lucas has fixed that latch on the gate yet?" Tyler asked Bigger. He turned, and the dog halted in his tracks, seeming not to wish to get any nearer than about six feet behind.

Tyler commenced walking again. Just because Bigger couldn't talk to him didn't mean he couldn't talk to Bigger.

"You know what Mama said, Bigger?" Tyler went on. "The same thing that almost everyone I know says—that Papa must be dead. She said that has to be the reason he hasn't come home yet." He continued walking, and listened for the dog's soft footfalls in the yellow dust behind him.

"What if she's right, Bigger?" he asked, and the question hung suspended on the cloudy morning air. "What if it's true that Papa's dead, that he's buried somewhere, will never come home again? What if he's gone forever, Bigger?"

Maybe it was a good thing that he could discuss this matter with Bigger; it was a subject that would be difficult to talk to a person about. *Dead. Buried. Never come home again. Gone forever.* Saying such words, looking at someone whose eyes might fill up with pity or horror, would be hard to do. Tyler turned again to consult Bigger.

The dog stopped, dropping his haunches into the dust as if he expected to hear more. "What dumb, stupid old Cousin Clayton said was even worse," Tyler muttered. "Why, of course Papa wants to be found!" At the mention of Clayton's name, Tyler was sure he saw the dog lift its left ear ever so slightly.

"Clayton doesn't know *I* know he'd have come with me in a minute if only I'd asked him," Tyler told Bigger. "He says I'm crazy as a cootie bug, that I'm daft—but he'd give anything to be as crazy as me. He'd like to quit being his mama's boy—only he can't work up enough nerve!"

This time when he continued his journey, Tyler imagined that the dog followed a little closer at his heels. "Bigger, you don't know Papa," Tyler explained, "so maybe you can't understand exactly why I've got to go find him." Tyler puzzled on it himself a moment.

Was it the sight and sound of Papa's lively eyes and rich, dark voice that he missed the most? Was it the fact that no one came around the farm on Sweet Creek when Papa wasn't there, that life wasn't jolly when there was no guffawing and backslapping and storytelling? Or was it because even a quick touch now and then of Papa's hand on his shoulder made him feel, well, like a son had a right to feel?

Tyler fished one of Papa's letters out of his pocket and

read a few lines to Bigger as he walked along. "No one knows how long this war will last," Papa wrote, "but the way some of our men can fight, why, I ought to be home in no time! Those boys in blue can't match our men in gray, especially when it comes to cavalry. Didn't they know us Missourians were born on horseback?"

Tyler refolded the letter and returned it to his shirt pocket. Papa's words were so full of hope and high spirits that Tyler was infected with confidence, too. "With Papa home, Bigger, things will be right again, just like Lucas says. I can go fishing more often with Lucas because I won't have to do most of the work myself. We can hunt squirrels, and maybe I can even spend more time with my books than I do now."

That sounded selfish and smallhearted, so Tyler amended his remark. "Not that I mind work, Bigger. Why, I've kept up the place in a way that'll make Papa proud." He remembered the loose hinge on the gate, and wished he'd taken time to fix it himself so things would be almost perfect when Papa got home.

Yet the possibility that *dead, buried, gone forever* nevertheless might turn out to be true haunted Tyler. "So what if that's how it is, Bigger?" he whispered. "That Papa's dead, that I'll never see him again—what will I do then?" He wished the dog would come even closer, would poke its wet nose into the palm of his hand like Maggie did when she wanted some loving.

Tyler noticed the dog's tail made a single quarter-sweep in the dust, like the hand on a clock going from twelve noon to a quarter past. "What will I do if Papa's dead, like everyone says?" Tyler asked again, this time softly, as if not saying the words too loud would keep such a thing from coming true.

If that's how it turns out to be, you'll make do somehow, the cool blue eye advised him.

Meantime, have faith, and don't imagine the worst before you know the best, the warm brown eye soothed.

Tyler smiled. Yes, that was good counsel, he decided. "So, Bigger, tell me about yourself," he invited, feeling expansive and relieved, in spite of the fact the dog hadn't said anything at all.

"Who was it that tied you up and left you in New Hope, Bigger? If you'd been *my* dog, why, I'd never have done that to you, cross my heart." Tyler turned so the dog could see him cross his heart. It seemed to him that Bigger hustled a bit, trotted a little closer behind than anytime before.

"When the three of us—you and me and Papa—finally get back home, you'll never be put on a chain again, Bigger. Nossir, you won't. Nobody'll ever say they're gonna take you out to the woods to put a bullet through your head either. And when we get back to Sweet Creek you'll have more than just people for company. We've got a fine hound there, Maggie's her name, and her four pups will torment the daylights out of you. You can be a good uncle to them, same's Uncle Matt is to me."

The scene was so warm in his mind—the vision of the two dogs on the hearth, the four fat pups rolling close by, Mama flushed and happy, Papa at the table with Lucas and Rosa Lee hanging on him—that the sound of the rock whizzing through the air and the sharp pain as it struck his right forehead caught Tyler totally unaware.

He reeled. He felt himself pitch backward. The earth

seemed to rotate in the opposite direction from the way he was falling. A roar filled his ears. Star bursts of red and yellow showered inside his head. The blow tumbled him flat in the road and left him spread-eagled in the dust as if it was he who'd been killed, not Oat Snepp's brother Billy.

☆ 8 ☆

WHEN TYLER CAME AROUND, HE FOUND HIMSELF STARING into a face that scared him worse than those in nightmares he used to have.

Looming above him were two narrow, slitted eyes. A pair of black brows as thick and furry as caterpillars. A cap of wild hair. Two blistered, dark lips parted to show a row of teeth, one of them in front badly chipped. A ragged, angry red scar shot like a lightning bolt from under the creature's left eye to the corner of its mouth.

Tyler blinked. The face came closer. He blinked again. Pain and terror nailed him to the ground. Instead of looking evil, though, the boy who crouched above him appeared to be even more frightened than he was himself.

"White b-b-b-boy, it wuz an a-a-a-accident," were the first words that came stammering out of that chipped-tooth mouth. "I din't heave that rock at you a purpose. Nossir, I surely din't!" Tyler could see that the boy leaning over him was as dark as Henry, Uncle Matt's livery hand, and wasn't much older than he was himself.

Tyler struggled to sit, and felt the other boy's wide, flat hand between his shoulder blades, helping him up. "Accident?" he heard himself mumble groggily. The shower of red and yellow star bursts in his head slowed to a drizzle. "I was just walking along, talking to my dog, when all of a sudden out of nowhere—" He glanced around. "Where's Bigger?" he demanded, his voice choked. "Doggone it, what'd you do with my dog?"

"Dog? Din't see no dog wit' you, white boy. I came runnin' as soon as I saw you go down in the road. For sure I'd a seen a dog if there'd a been one. Nossir, din't see no dog a tall." The stranger drew his brows together, and peered at Tyler with a sidelong glance. "You say you wuz—*talkin'* to this here dog?"

"Bigger—dog's named Bigger," Tyler muttered weakly, his head throbbing. He felt sick to his stomach, as if he might throw up his breakfast. "He's been traveling with me. I better try to find—"

"Take it easy, white boy. Maybe he jus' took off not meaning to stay away for long. Might a skeered him to see you topple over in the road like you wuz a tree somebody'd just chopped down. If he's a good dog I wager he'll show up again real quick, checkin' to see if you is all right."

Tyler staggered to his feet, then stood swaying in the sullen morning air. The stranger steadied him. "They's a bad, clotty little spot on your fo'head, white boy. Better you come over here and let me wash you up."

His eyes didn't seem to focus quite right, so Tyler let himself be led under some low trees near a marshy pond, where he half sat, half fell to the ground. The stranger squatted beside him, then began to sponge at his forehead with a scrap of cloth he tore off the end of his own shirt. "This here be any worse, white boy, and you'd be playin' pretty music with a band of angels right now," he observed with a chuckle.

"What were you trying to do, anyhow?" Tyler groaned. It made him downright peeved to realize the other boy believed there was something humorous about the situation. He flopped back on the points of his elbows to study the stranger more carefully. There, on the ground beside the black boy, Tyler spied a slingshot. It was made of oak, its stout handle worn smooth and shiny by long use.

"That what you tried to kill me with?" Tyler growled, pointing to it and staring the stranger square in the eye. "Most black folks I know don't have one of those."

"It's rightfully mine," the other boy answered gruffly. "Made it myself a long time back, and I was fixin' to ketch me a rabbit for supper. I seen a big one hoppin' crost this here road jus' before I saw you, case you think it's any a your bizness."

Tyler rubbed his head. The lump above his eye felt as big as an apple. "I sure didn't see no rabbit," he muttered.

"Course not," the stranger retorted, "cuz you be so busy *talkin'* to that dog you claim to be travelin' wit'." The boy gave Tyler a sly look. "Now what I want to know is— does that dog talk back to you?"

Tyler glowered, then crawled to his feet. He still felt groggy, and his companion cautioned, "Don't hasten on your way if you ain't up to it yet. Mebbe you ought to rest here in the shade wit' me a while longer."

Tyler shook his head. "Got to look for Bigger," he insisted. "Got a far piece to travel. Got no time to waste

64

sitting around in the shade talking to someone who just tried to kill me."

"Where you be headed?"

"Mexico."

"Mexico! I think I heard a that place once. Yessir, I think mebbe I did. What you aim to do when you get there, anyways?"

"I'm looking for my pa." To say *papa* would make it sound as if he were a child not much older than Lucas. "I think he's ailing, and might need help getting back home," he explained.

"Mexico mus' be a mighty big place. Where do you aim to begin this here lookin'?"

"Down along the Rio Grande. Someone told me Pa might be headed that way."

"Well, if it won't bother you none I'll walk along with you a spell. Not all the way to Mexico, a course. Only till I get to Tuttle, 'bout two-three days travel from here."

For the second time Tyler tried to observe the stranger without appearing to be too nosy. The other boy was slightly taller and even leaner than he was himself, wore a thin blue cotton shirt, trousers that were fastened at the waist with a belt two sizes too long, and no shoes.

It was a mighty light way to travel, Tyler mused, hoisting his pack to his shoulders. He was about to ask the other boy why he hadn't packed more than the clothes on his back when Bigger came trotting around the edge of the marsh. He carried a rabbit in his mouth.

"Why, looka that!" the black boy exclaimed, clapping his knee with delight. "That the dog you were talkin' about—and talkin' to? Why, I do b'leeve he ketched my rabbit for me!"

"*Your* rabbit?" Tyler countered, his own voice cool. He felt determination heat his blood. "That's my dog, mister, which means that must be *my* rabbit!" Bigger, looking pleased with himself, dropped his trophy in the grass. The moment he saw the stranger, however, Tyler saw the dog curl his lip, heard a familiar warning growl rumble up from his bibbed white chest.

The other boy stepped aside, dropped his glance, then lifted one shoulder in a rueful shrug. "So it's your rabbit," he agreed in a tired, flat voice. "You take it. Anyway, *I'm* the one who oughta be movin' along—"

"No, wait." Tyler stayed him with a raised palm. Something in the other boy's quick surrender made him ashamed of himself. The rabbit was good-sized, plenty big enough to share. "We'll divvy it up fair and square," he offered. "I've got a knife we can skin it with. You be the one to roast it up. Half for you, half for me, the bones for Bigger. Fair?"

The black boy eyed him carefully before he nodded. "Fair," he finally agreed. "But best you do the gutting right now, white boy. Meat'll keep better that way," he advised, picking the rabbit out of the grass as soon as Bigger slunk away. Tyler dug his knife out of his pocket, took the rabbit, then cleaned it as quickly as he'd have done at home. He tossed the steaming entrails out to Bigger, who wolfed them down while keeping a hostile eye fastened on the newcomer.

"We won't roast it up until evening, though," Tyler said. He wiped his knife against some leaves. "You meant what you said about going in my direction? We might as well get moving, then."

*　*　*

66

That night, the roasted rabbit was excellent, though Tyler decided it would've been tastier with a little salt, something both Mama and Aunt Margaret forgot to remind him to take along. After the fire had been banked Tyler stretched himself on one side of it, while the other boy stretched out on the opposite edge.

Tyler passed his hand over his forehead. A loud ringing persisted in his ears, and the knot above his eye was still warm and tender even though a crusty scab now covered the wound.

"White boy, you awake over there?" came a voice from across the fire.

"Yep—but if you and me aim to travel together all the way to Tuttle you can't go on calling me white boy—and truth to tell I don't fancy calling you black boy," Tyler mumbled sleepily. "Best we own up to our real names. Mine's Tyler. My pa is Black Jack Bohannon; during the war he rode with General Jo Shelby of the Iron Cavalry Brigade of Missouri."

There was a brief silence on the other side of the fire. The stranger was thinking, Tyler realized, that if Papa had ridden with Shelby it meant he stood for slavery. "Mine's Isaac Peerce," the other boy said at last. "I'm named after my daddy. He—that first Isaac Peerce—he got sold away before I had a chance to make his acquaintance."

Sold? Somehow, that word sounded hard and closed on the mild, dusky spring air. Sold, as when Papa took a calf to market? Sold, as when Mama sometimes took eggs into McMinnville? But why do I feel surprised? Tyler asked himself. That's the way it usually was if you were a black person, wasn't it?

Uncle Matt had bought Henry when he went on busi-

67

ness once over to Kentucky, said he was real proud of the bargain he got on him, too. But when Mr. Lincoln decided it wasn't fitting for one man to own another, when he signed the Emancipation Proclamation that declared henceforth it would be the law of the land for people of color to be free, Uncle Matt told Henry he was. Now Henry worked for a wage, wasn't always at somebody's beck and call, told to do this, go there, fetch that. Henry had a house of his own out behind the livery stable, had a door on it that he could lock when he felt like it. Sometimes he didn't answer when someone knocked. "Don't have to if it don't suit me," Henry would call out, with no apology in his voice.

"Yessir, sold," Isaac assured Tyler. "He belonged to Mr. Curwood, who was master to both my mama and my daddy. My mama said my daddy was a fine-looking man but Mr. Curwood needed money mighty bad one year when the crops wuz poor. He be a gamblin' man, see, and had to pay a debt he owed. Let my daddy go for eight hunert dollars, Mama tol' me."

From the other side of the fire, Isaac Peerce's voice became more pensive than ever. "I never laid eyes on my daddy—but I do b'leeve any man worth eight hunert dollars must a been quite a man!"

It was Tyler's turn to be silent. Here I am, looking for Papa, but yonder's Isaac, who doesn't even know what his father looks like. Wouldn't recognize him if he passed by him in the road tomorrow. Doesn't know if his papa is dead or alive or if he'll ever meet him in his life.

"So you've never seen your papa—*ever?*" Tyler asked, hoping Isaac owned some small memory he could treasure of that first Isaac Peerce. What if he himself had never known Papa? Oh, how poor he'd be!

"Never did," Isaac admitted. "I was still in my mama's belly when he got sold away to a far place no one remembers the name of now."

"Do you ever wonder—" Tyler began, then didn't quite know how to finish. Do you ever wonder if you look like him, if he's everything your mama claimed he was? had been the question he'd intended to ask.

"Yes, I do. All the time," Isaac whispered. "Someday, maybe when I least 'spect it, I'll meet a man somewhere and it'll turn out his name's same as mine. He'll be a proud man, and won't bow down to nobody. It's possible, now that we black folk are free." He paused. "Possible, but not likely, I guess," he confessed. "Only it's this dream I have in my head, white boy, and I ain't turning loose of it!"

"So call me Tyler," Tyler reminded him, "and I'll call you Isaac, all right?"

"Yessir, that'd be fine. Me callin' you that and you callin' me t'other," the boy on the opposite side of the fire agreed. The coals died down to a mere glow, and Tyler felt his eyes grow heavier. Today he'd been knocked out with a stone that'd come out of nowhere like a cannonball to dang near kill him. Had met a boy named Isaac Peerce, who wore a terrible scar, who wasn't exactly looking for his father, just hoping someday, accidentally, he might run onto him. Bigger had chased down a rabbit; roasted, it had been tasty, even without salt. Yes, it had been a full day.

Just before he went to sleep Tyler felt something press

69

against his flank. He reached out sleepily, to bury his fingers against a shoulder covered with fur as thick as a bear cub's. Bigger pressed his nose into the boy's palm. Never before had the dog come so close.

Tyler smiled into the darkness, and caressed the dog's silky ears. They were as soft as he'd imagined they'd be. Across the fire Tyler heard Isaac begin to snore softly, and with his fingers locked in Bigger's fur, he slept, too.

☆9☆

WHEN THEY SET OUT AFTER BREAKFAST BIGGER STAYED farther back than usual, his head held low, as if in the clear light of morning he was ashamed to remember he'd slept snugged up tight as a tick the night before.

"That dog a yourn ain't none too friendly," Isaac observed as they walked along. He glanced over his shoulder in Bigger's direction, and when he did Tyler saw that the jagged scar on the other boy's cheek looked pink rather than scarlet in the pale morning light. "Might be somebody beat on him real good sometime or t'other," Isaac speculated.

"That's what I figured myself," Tyler admitted. "Pa told me it was the quickest way to the ruination of a good dog."

"Yep, I reckon that be so," Isaac agreed. After a moment's pause, he added quietly, "Dogs ain't the only ones t'be ruined that way. Bein' beat on can make a body mean."

Tyler wondered if it was a beating that had given the other boy a mark branding him with a lightning bolt from his eye to the corner of his mouth. He was on the verge of asking when Isaac lifted his fingers to his own face and slowly traced the scar from top to bottom.

"Mr. Curwood, he got mighty peeved wit' me one day, and laid my cheek open till Mama said she could see the bone in there, all shiny white and spooky." Isaac sounded as if he were still amazed at what had happened. "My grandma closed it up as bes' she could wit' rags and a potion made up out a bacon grease and chamomile. I tell you, it hurt real smart for a while!"

"You must've done something pretty bad for him to whup you like that," Tyler suggested carefully, unable to imagine what would make a grown man strike a boy so hard he'd bare the flesh to the bone, leaving a mark such as the one Isaac would have to wear till the end of his days.

"I had to move my bowels," Isaac explained, "and went out a the field toward the woods to do so. Made Mr. Curwood awful mad, I can tell you! 'You there, Isaac!' he holler t'me in a voice louder'n a whole passle a church bells. 'You drop your drawers only when *I* tell you to, not a minute before and not a minute after! You hear me talkin' t'you, boy?' Guess I din't pull my britches up quick enough, cuz he come over t'me and laid my face open wit' the butt end of his riding stick. My, Isaac never fret overmuch 'bout his bowels ever again!" he exclaimed, and laughed, not cheerfully, but as if he continued to marvel at the sudden swiftness of that punishment.

When Isaac smiled Tyler noticed again that a tooth in front had a corner knocked off it. He decided he didn't want to hear how that had happened. Sometimes, well, maybe it was better not to know too much. Just the same, it made a hard knot in Tyler's chest to know Isaac's face had been laid open because a gambling man lost his temper. He'd have liked it better, he decided, if he knew Papa had been against such things as happened to people like Isaac. Maybe it wasn't enough not to own a slave yourself, as Papa once claimed.

"We're going to be mighty hungry come nightfall," Tyler said, eager to change the subject. "We're going to have to figure out a way to get ourselves some new victuals."

"We surely are," Isaac agreed. "Quickest thing to do right off would be to fish."

"We got nothing to string a pole with," Tyler pointed out. "Mighty hard to fish without any line."

Isaac gave him a superior smile. "You think I'd a left home without takin' me some twine? Not likely!" He reached into his pants pocket, and took out a length of twine that had been wrapped carefully around a twig, figure-eight style, to keep it from getting snarled. With thumb and forefinger Isaac dug in his shirt to retrieve a small, barbed hook. "What you're lookin' at here, white boy, is supper for tonight," he said with another grin.

"You're not s'posed to call me white boy anymore," Tyler reminded him.

Isaac nodded, which Tyler took to be an apology. He loaned the other boy his knife, and watched as Isaac cut a willow pole from a small grove near the creek. "You go off there in the grass and catch me a couple of nice little green grasshoppers," Isaac suggested. "In springtime, oh them greenies, they make mighty fine bait for trout."

Fifteen minutes later Isaac pulled a wriggling, speckled, ten-inch, rainbow-sided trout out of the stream. It was followed a few moments later by another one almost as big.

"Let me have a go," Tyler asked, and then it was his turn to catch a pair of fish that almost but not quite equaled Isaac's in size.

"Double that, Ty Bohannon, and we got ourselves a meal," Isaac said, cutting a willow fork to carry the fish on until suppertime.

That night they feasted on fish held on sticks over the fire until they were blackened and sizzling hot. Bigger was awarded the heads, and Tyler donated his last two apples to complete the meal.

"What's going to happen now?" Tyler wondered aloud. "Oh sure, tomorrow maybe we can fish again. I got a tin of meat we can share. Then, if Bigger can catch us another rabbit—" Tyler let his words trail away. "Truth is, Isaac, I never figured it'd be so—"

"So hard, scrounging ever' livelong day for food?" Isaac filled in softly.

"Yeah, I suppose that's what I mean all right," Tyler confessed, staring into the fire.

"Last year a the war, livin' got mighty hard where I came from," Isaac murmured. "Babies and old folks, they die real regular. Master Curwood—well, he took a notion the Union was going to win—so he turn all us black folks loose. 'Don't own you no more, don't have to feed you or put you up neither!' he tol' us one day. We'd been hopin' for freedom, but freedom with nothin' to eat, no roof over our heads—no, it wasn't such a grand thing as we figured it'd be. It take a mighty lot of diggin' in the fields to come up with one onion or maybe two carrots to feed the lot of us. It's one a the reasons now ol' Isaac is travelin', to find himself a better place to be."

"Did you have to leave your mama behind?" Tyler asked.

Isaac was silent for a brief moment. "She be gone," he answered softly. "And my grandma and granddaddy too."

"You mean—they're all—dead?" Tyler tried to imagine the lonesomeness of not having any kin of your own left. What if something happened to the three he'd left back there at Sweet Creek? He'd have no home of his own anymore, might have to go live with Uncle Matt. He'd never be the oldest again, he'd only be second best. Clayton would see to that.

"Yessir, they be all gone," Isaac replied.

It will be hard work to find Papa, Tyler realized, but Isaac doesn't even have anyone left to look for, except a man he might not recognize even if he finds him. It was an awful fate, and he searched his mind for something to say to the other boy. "Someday maybe it will all be different, Isaac," were the only words that came to him.

"Yessir, mebbe someday it will." Isaac sighed. Tyler sneaked a peek at his companion across the fire, expecting to see the other boy's dark eyes shiny with tears. Instead, Isaac seemed solemn and resigned. Only the scar, bright now in the firelight, registered anger and indignation.

"Country's beginnin' to look familiar to these tired eyes," Isaac announced two days later when they approached the Tuttle River. "I came this way once with Mr. Cur-

75

wood. He brought us along to do the unloading of a boat that came up carrying rope and leather. I was only a tad back then."

"How old're you now?" Tyler wanted to know.

The question surprised Isaac. His eyes got round beneath his fuzzy caterpillar brows. "How old? Why, I don't know for sure! Mebbe about—about your age, I think. How old are *you*?"

"Twelve," Tyler answered.

"Stand up here!" Isaac ordered, picking a stick out of the road. "Let's see how we measure, shoulder to shoulder." Tyler stood up straight, and could feel Isaac's shoulder blades and buttocks pressed against his own. Isaac laid the stick across their two shoulders, tried to hold it level, then peered down while Tyler did the same. It was plain Isaac's shoulder was higher by more than an inch.

Isaac jumped aside, and did a nimble jig in the road. "Mus' mean I'm older'n you be!" he sang out. "That might make me almost . . ." He hesitated.

"Thirteen." Tyler supplied the number for him.

Isaac put his finger to his chin and marveled. "Thirteen. I'll remember that," he promised. "And next year, wherever I be, at a time of year when the sun looks 'bout the same in the sky as it does right now, I'll be able to say I'm . . ."

"Fourteen," Tyler provided.

"Fourteen," Isaac whispered. "Why, I'll almost be a man."

Almost a man. Tyler had never thought of himself in such a way. He was Black Jack Bohannon's son, still only a boy. But soon, like Isaac, he'd be a man himself. He'd still be his father's son, but something more: He'd have

76

to decide important things, would be even more responsible than he was now.

After they crossed the Tuttle River, Isaac turned to face Tyler. "Guess this is where we got to go different ways," he said. "Before she died, my mama told me I'd find shelter down there with folks she'd known a long time back." He pointed through the trees. He didn't hurry away, though. Instead, he brushed his feet back and forth in the yellow dust, and seemed to have something on his mind.

Tyler wondered if they ought to shake hands. It would be the decent thing to do; he'd shaken hands with Uncle Matt, and even would have shaken Clayton's plump mitt if that little mama's boy hadn't insisted on staring at the points of his shoes as if he saw a prince's reflection down there. Before he could decide what to do, Isaac held out the fishing pole he'd made the second day they traveled together.

"You take this here rig, Ty," he said. "I can get me more twine if I needs it from those folks who'll take me in. This'll help you feed yourself as you travel all the way down there to Mexico."

It was a fine parting gift, Tyler realized, one that he'd be thankful for many times over. He took the pole gratefully. "Thank you kindly, Isaac," he mumbled. Tyler wished there was something he could give the other boy that would matter, something that would make life as much easier as the pole would make his own. Isaac brushed his bare feet in the dust again, then turned to go.

"Hold on a minute," Tyler commanded, and set his pack in the road. He opened it up, and fished out the shoes he'd packed inside. "These are for you. Take 'em, Isaac."

"My stars," Isaac whispered. "A pair a shoes! Might be too little for these big ol' feet, though." He knelt down and put them on. "Nossir, they feel fine." He studied Tyler doubtfully. "Isaac don't have far to go, though. You got miles to travel yet, Ty Bohannon." He pulled his feet out of the shoes and held them out. "Better you take 'em back. They be too good to give away to the likes a me."

Tyler tied up his pack. "No, they're yours now, Isaac. You got traveling to do, same as me."

Isaac nodded; his chipped-tooth smile was shy. He put the shoes back on, laced them up. "Good luck," he said. "I hope you find your daddy."

"Good luck to you, too," Tyler echoed. "Now the war's over, I hope you'll get to meet that other Isaac Peerce someday," he added. He watched as Isaac walked down the road and descended the hill toward a patch of trees. There, Isaac Peerce turned, and waved for a long, long time.

Tyler had thought it would be easy to part, that Isaac hadn't mattered much. After all, they'd only traveled together four days. He was a black boy, not someone like Oat Snepp, who'd been a chum since they started going to Mr. Blackburn's school together.

But Isaac and me are more alike than we are different, Tyler realized. Both Isaac and me are looking for our fathers, Isaac not looking too hard yet, me figuring I know just where I'll find mine. Tyler waved, squinting until Isaac became small, smaller, only a speck, then vanished completely.

"Good luck, Isaac," he called again, softly, glad he'd given him the shoes. "Why, it's a queer thing, Bigger," he murmured, surprised. "Till this morning I didn't know it could make a person feel better to give something away than to hang on to it." Bigger listened attentively, and in the yellow dust his tail marked off another quarter hour.

☆ 10 ☆

With Isaac gone, once again there was no one to talk to but Bigger.

Tyler smiled to remember that Isaac had asked, his voice incredulous: "You say you wuz—*talkin'* to this here dog?" Later, the look in his eye half sly, half suspicious, he'd wanted to know, "Does that dog talk back to you?"

Tyler turned to study Bigger himself. "If you could talk, Bigger, what kind of stories would you tell me?" he wondered out loud. Now that it was just the two of them again, Bigger seemed more willing to walk almost at his heel, even in broad daylight. When they made camp each night the dog sat so close beside him, in front of the fire, that once sparks nearly singed his muslin bib.

At the first campsite they made after Isaac walked away, the grass was thick enough that Tyler didn't need to make a pallet of boughs. When he stretched himself out with a sigh, Bigger once again laid against his side, flank to flank.

Tyler reached out to stroke the dog's big head. "Won't be long until we cross over into Arkansas," he murmured

80

into the darkness. The fire died down, and its rosy glow no longer lighted the underside of the canopy of leaves above his head. "We're getting closer, Bigger, closer all the time to finding Papa."

Tyler thought about the X's he'd made on his paper. There were eight of them already, which meant he must've covered almost two hundred forty miles. He always deducted a few miles from the total count, though, because he knew some days he didn't walk as steadily as other days, such as when he'd been so groggy after the blow Isaac had accidentally given him.

It would take perhaps fifteen days to travel the length of Arkansas, and arrive at the Texas border. Traveling across Texas in mid-June might be perilously hot, as Uncle Matt had predicted. But he couldn't worry about that now; the only thing that mattered was getting all the way down to the Rio Grande. When Tyler studied his map, though, it was plain that the river covered the entire southwestern border of Texas. *Where,* exactly, along that snakelike line, would he be most likely to find Papa? What had seemed like a solid plan many days ago at home now seemed shaky and uncertain.

As he looked up at the stars, the boy soothed himself by imagining what was going on back at Sweet Creek. Maggie's pups would have their eyes open by now, soon would be eating table scraps, not wearing their mama down with constant suckling. Lucas ought to have culti-vated the corn again; the beans would have blossomed; the squash would already be the size of pullet eggs. Mama would be thinking of weaning Calico's calf, would keep it in a separate stall at night, then in a corner of the upland pasture during the day.

81

And what about Cousin Clayton? Tyler grinned sleepily. He wished he had a way to send Clayton a letter and tell him about some of the things he'd done. How he'd slept out every night under the stars, had almost been killed by a blow to his head, that he and a boy named Isaac had roasted a whole rabbit over a fire. But that would be spiteful. Clayton wouldn't want to hear such news. Staying at home with his mama was punishment enough; there was no need to rub salt into his wounds.

Thinking of letters, though, made Tyler decide to read a few lines from one of Papa's before he got any sleepier and the fire was too dim to see by. The longer he was gone from home, the more need he had of the reassurance he always got from Papa's words. It was as if he could hear Black Jack's voice float off the page, could see the expression in his black eyes.

Tyler sat up, pulled the letter from his pocket, and, squinting in the dull light, began to read aloud to Bigger.

"It's not that I'm personally fond of slavery," Papa wrote. "It ain't that I want to put another man in chains myself. Nossir, that's not the reason I've thrown my lot with these boys in gray." Tyler read slowly, remembering the lightning bolt on Isaac's cheek. He'd read this passage before, but now, having heard the story Isaac told about Mr. Curwood's bad temper, Papa's words sounded different.

"You see, what sticks in my craw like a bone is those chaps up there in Washington thinking they can dictate to us out here how we ought to run our business. Do we tell those Yankees how to run their railroads? How to count the money in their banks? Why no, we don't! That's why I'm fighting this war, so I can run my own show, and

82

my neighbor can run his, neither one of us telling t'other one how to do the job."

Yes, in a way Papa's words made sense, Tyler agreed, narrowing his eyes and staring into the fire. Yet what about a man such as Mr. Curwood, who thought nothing of punishing a boy like Isaac over the whens and whys of relieving his bowels in the woods?

Tyler regretted having such a disloyal thought, but now he wondered: Was it possible that Uncle Matt was more right than Papa was? Uncle Matt believed that slavery itself had to go, that it couldn't be a choice anymore, that nobody ever ought to have the right to put another man or woman in chains like a dog.

"What do *you* think?" Tyler asked, leaning toward Bigger. After all, Bigger knew very well what it was like to be in chains.

I'm not a devil; I only show my teeth when I'm scared, Bigger's brown eye answered.

On moonlit nights I knew I'd be free some day; now I am, the blue eye replied.

Well, if that's how Bigger felt, think how it must've been for Isaac and his mama and his daddy, Tyler reasoned. Isaac's daddy had been sold away, never to know if the wife he left behind had given birth to a son or a daughter. Would never know that the child born was a boy who'd been named after him, a boy who'd had his cheek laid open with the butt end of a gambling man's riding stick. Later, Tyler hoped, when he and Papa were on their way home, they could talk about this. By now Papa most likely had changed his mind about a lot of things. Maybe about slavery, too.

* * *

It was late afternoon when Tyler crested a rise on what was called Telegraph Road on his scrap of map, and came upon the field.

It was uncommonly green, so vast and wide he could scarcely see all the way across to where it met the edge of the blue horizon. On one side was a peach orchard, heavy brush along another, the brow of a hill rising on the south.

In the far distance, the boy could make out several figures. He shaded his eyes; four or five men were working with spades, turning up the sod. It was late to be getting the land ready to plant crops, Tyler thought, frowning. The war being finished so recently, maybe nobody'd had time to do any field work till now.

"We'll ask 'em how far we are from the Texas border, Bigger," Tyler announced, hurrying across the vast green expanse that spread before him like a smooth carpet. "Looks to me like they're no strangers to these parts, and will be able to help us out." *Us*—the word had a comfortable sound, and Tyler noticed that Bigger wagged his tail agreeably, his ears lifted, as they hurried to where the men were working.

When he got nearer Tyler saw the men weren't exactly turning the sod over. No. They were digging graves.

Laid out on the green grass all around, Tyler saw the long, white bones of dead men's legs . . . shorter ones of men's arms and hands . . . several skulls, smooth as globes . . . segments of spine, delicate as knucklebones . . . scraps of cloth, blue and gray all mixed together . . . belt buckles, buttons, several pairs of eyeglasses in a pile . . . in another pile shoes, a few of them hardly worn, dented canteens, crumpled caps, a small, mildewed book with writing in it, a cracked photograph of a dark-haired lady in a white dress.

Tyler slowed his pace. It seemed an act of poor manners to stare at what was laid out right before his eyes. *The bodies were piled like cordwood,* the old woman had told him, but he hadn't wanted to believe her.

One of the diggers leaned on his spade, a man not young anymore, his face covered with a patchy gray beard. He turned when he heard footsteps behind him. "What you lookin' for way out here, sonny?" he demanded roughly, his voice weary.

"I'm traveling," Tyler answered. "I'm searching for my pa."

"Maybe he's one of these here chaps." One of graybeard's companions guffawed, touching a nearby skull lightly with the tip of his shovel. The moment he raised the shovel, a low, rumbling growl came out of Bigger, and the man lowered it hastily. Tyler was surprised, too. Only a moment ago, Bigger had been cheerful, had been wagging his back end as happily as Maggie did on her way to a squirrel hunt.

"What's wrong with that dog, boy?" the man grumbled. "Doggone mutt's giving me a look like he wants to take my hand off at the elbow!"

"Forget the dog," graybeard warned, glaring at his fellow gravedigger. "No need to scare the lad *or* his hairy pal."

Tyler hesitated. "What are you doing?" he asked, hoping the question didn't sound ignorant. "If these men were buried, why are you digging 'em up and burying 'em all over again?"

"They were all in a pile in a trench, sonny. When an army moves off a battlefield in the middle of a war there's no time to bury the dead politely, each man to his own private spot."

Ah. So the old woman had been right about that, too.

"I'm pretty sure my pa ain't dead," Tyler murmured, touching the three letters in his breast pocket. Yet these men, whose flesh has rotted off their bones, were likely fathers to boys like me or brothers to boys like Oat Snepp, he realized.

"Pa was one of the first in Caldwell County to pledge to Jeff Davis," Tyler blurted, as if the words guaranteed Black Jack Bohannon himself couldn't possibly be dead.

Graybeard rolled his eyes. "Not necessarily a smart choice," he said. "They got ol' Jeff Davis in solitary confinement over there in Fortress Monroe, Virginia. Got irons on his wrists and ankles as if he was any common thief. Your pa would a done a whole lot better for himself, sonny, to have gone over to those chaps in the blueberry-colored suits."

"They captured President Davis?" Tyler echoed.

"Yessir, they surely did. Down there in a patch of woods near Irwinville, Georgia. Them Union boys ran him down like a dog."

When the stranger had stopped at Sweet Creek, he obviously hadn't known what President Davis's fate had been any more than he'd known about President Lincoln's. Tyler was almost afraid to ask about Jo Shelby, but forced himself to put the question to the men who looked at him with what he knew was pity.

"You heard any word about General Shelby?" he whispered, dreading what the news might be.

Graybeard chortled. "Well now, ain't he a man to draw

to!" He shifted his weight against his shovel, eager to interrupt the job he'd been doing.

"Heard a story about him the other day. Listen: Shelby commandeered three whole wagonloads of food from the Federals—rice, beans, flour, cornmeal, coffee—his rebs won't go hungry, that's for sure! He's headed for a place called Eagle Pass, on the border between Texas and Mexico. Says no fool Yankee will take him alive!" The gravedigger's small eyes were bright with grudging respect. "Who can tell, maybe your pa is with Shelby, not in jail like poor ol' Jeff Davis."

As he listened, glad for the news, something about the spot where he stood nibbled at Tyler's thoughts. "This place," he asked, glancing about, "was it one of the big battlefields?"

"Not like Gettysburg or Antietam or Shiloh, where men stuck wads of cotton in their ears to cut the sound of the guns and got killed by tens of hundreds—but big enough. This here's Pea Ridge, young feller. The Union won in the end, but lemme ask you: What kind of victory is it when more than a thousand men on each side go down? Same thing happened at Wilson's Creek. Sure, that time it was the rebs who carried the day—but more'n a thousand boys on each side fell there too."

As he spoke a look came into graybeard's eye that reminded Tyler of the expression in the stranger's that night at Sweet Creek. Such men seemed to have seen too much, to have looked on sights they couldn't unsee or unremember.

The old man pointed to the row of skulls. "Look at them," he ordered, his voice brusque, and Tyler found himself staring in spite of himself. The skulls lying scattered in the green grass, stripped clean of flesh and hair, were smaller than Tyler imagined grown men's would be, and looked so alike he couldn't tell one from the other.

"That's right, sonny—no way to know now if their uniforms were blue or gray, is there?" graybeard demanded. "No way to know if they were fat or lean, had blue eyes or brown. Dead, all men look alike. These chaps are brothers now, whether they aimed to be in life or not."

A feeling came over Tyler that was not one he'd have called sad or mournful. It was much larger, more complex than that. It sucked the spirit right out of him. He looked up at the sky, away from the green field in which the crowns of dead men's skulls blossomed like pale, round flowers.

Overhead the dome of the world was silent, empty save for an occasional hawk or a drifting cloud. It was obscene to know that when he lowered his eyes he'd again bear witness to the clean, white bones of arms and legs, the strange, permanent smiles fixed on skulls scattered in the grass.

"I got to be going," he muttered, barely able to get the words out, turning away without asking how far it was to Texas.

"Grab yourself a pair a them shoes if you need 'em," graybeard invited, pointing at one of the piles. Tyler snatched up a pair, remembering that he didn't have extra ones now that he'd given his others to Isaac. He didn't take time to say good-bye to the gravediggers. If he lingered, graybeard might decide to tell him more he didn't want to hear.

By the time he reached the edge of the green field,

Tyler was running as hard as he could, the dead man's shoes slapping against his hip as he flew, a name burning in his brain: *Eagle Pass.*

That night Tyler read hungrily from one of Papa's letters again. He had to bring Papa nearer, to reread words he'd already read dozens of times, to make sure he wasn't dead like those men being reburied in the peaceful green field on Pea Ridge. He read the words hungrily, as if they were fresh:

"It's a strange thing," Papa wrote, "but a big part of war is not having much to do. We've been camped for many days in a pretty woods with a fine stream running through it. Nearby, our horses have good pasture for grazing." The scene he painted was so unlike the ones the gravedigger had spoken of that it was as if the old man and Papa spoke of different wars.

"Wife, tell sons Ty and Lucas I've learned a fine new game; the boys in the Brigade think it's a jolly way to spend an afternoon. It's called baseball, and I aim to teach fellers up and down Sweet Creek how to play it when I come home."

When I come home. There. Papa said it himself: *When I come home.* Tyler felt the four words nestle side by side in his heart, softer and sweeter than new-hatched robins in their mother's nest. Once again, Papa became a merry, laughing gypsy sort of man. Most important of all, he was *notdead, notdead, notdead.*

"Sometimes we play cards, other times it's marbles," Papa went on. "Ask Ty if he still has that aggie I brought home to him for his birthday a long time back. I think of you each day, Family, and pray that you all stay well."

Tyler refolded the letter, then fetched the aggie out of his pocket. "Just like your eye, Bigger," he said when Bigger moved closer. The fire glimmered through the aggie, turning it mauve instead of blue. "It's going to bring us luck, I just know it will. Long as we have this, we're sure to find Papa."

To know that Papa had learned a fine new game, that he remembered the aggie, soothed the ache in Tyler's heart. He wouldn't think about Pea Ridge anymore, about rusted belt buckles, bones as white as marble, or skulls that bloomed like strange flowers in the afternoon sun.

Perhaps Pea Ridge was an aberration, one of only a few fields where dead men had to be reburied. Tyler was glad Papa filled his letters instead with stories about learning new games, of generals with hearts like mountain lions, most of all of men who made it through their battles. He didn't want to think anymore about the ones who hadn't.

☆ 11 ☆

In Texas, Tyler skirted Lake O' the Pines, crossed the Sabine River by ferryboat near Mineola, later the Trinity not far from Cross Roads. When he studied his map he saw other rivers descending like rungs of a ladder on his way to Eagle Pass: the Brazos, the Colorado, the Pedernales. So many wild rivers to be crossed in a world once composed of a single small stream named Sweet Creek!

Tyler hoped he could remember the names of all the towns he passed through so he'd be able to tell Mama and Lucas: Mount Pleasant, Newsome, Quitman. Murchison, Corsicana, Dawson. McGregor, Belton, Burnet. Soon he couldn't remember in which order he'd passed through such places. Their names melted together in his mind. After a while, he couldn't recall what sight he'd seen in which town.

He bought a canteen, his first purchase with Uncle Matt's money. He splurged on a dozen tins of meat and a bag of hard biscuits, many of which turned out to be

91

wormy (Bigger ate them anyway). Soon the country he traveled across became flat and dry. The trees were short and scrubby, no longer casting cool umbrellas of shade. The lively creeks of the up-country gave way to thin, brown streams; fishing got poor. The earth was covered with chaparral that tore at his trousers. The days were hot, the nights astonishingly cold.

The sun was nailed daily like a brass plate in the fierce blue sky, and Tyler kept the kerchief Uncle Matt had given him tied high around his neck. The flat land was relieved now and then by gullies and washes that had been carved by the sudden heavy downpours of the desert country. He lay in the shady banks of such dry gullies during the hottest part of the day, then forced himself to walk late into the evening to be sure of making good mileage.

The going became hard in a new way: Tyler was wearier than he could ever remember being. He'd grown terribly thin; his collarbone stuck out; his hipbones were a pair of hooks his pants hung from. Once, as he bathed in a small stream, he noticed his chest was devoid of excess flesh, his ribs so prominent they could've been strummed like banjo strings. Often, there was a funny taste in his mouth, dry and metallic. Some nights his feet were so swollen he could hardly pull them out of the dead soldier's shoes (he'd started to wear them, as near as he could remember, when he went through a place called Prairie Hill).

*   *   *

He was too tired to talk to Bigger anymore. Bigger himself kept his head low, panting in the merciless heat. Boy and dog scarcely lifted their feet out of the dust, used no more energy than was needed barely to keep going. Tyler was too weary at night to read the letters in his pocket. The joy of getting closer to Papa faded, became like a dream he couldn't quite remember after waking in the morning.

Each time he went through a village or passed someone in a dusty road, Tyler asked about General Shelby. "He was headed this way," he explained, "and I think my father might be riding with him." The answer he got from strangers didn't vary much.

"No, son, nobody hereabouts has seen any bunch of soldiers such as ones like you're talkin' about." There would be a pause for some thoughtful head scratching. "Pretty hard for six hundred men to travel together and not be noticed, don't you reckon? Must be you're mistaken about 'em bein' headed down Texas way. They best be careful, though; General Phil Sheridan is lookin' for just such a bunch of fellers, too."

At Dripping Springs someone allowed he'd heard a bunch of men were holed up down in San Antonio, but when Tyler examined his map he realized that to check out the truth of the rumor he'd have to go at least sixty or eighty miles straight south—two or three days' worth of walking. Better to disregard talk of such sightings; better to head straight as an arrow for Eagle Pass.

*   *   *

When he knocked at doors along the way, sometimes he'd be lucky enough to get invited to stay for supper even without doing chores. "I'm not lookin' for any favors," he explained, "but I'd sure appreciate a meal if you can spare one." Folks in Texas ate differently than folks in Missouri, Tyler soon discovered. So many beans! Red, black, white, calico—often cooked with rice, then made spicy with red and green chilies that he wasn't used to. He longed for some of Aunt Margaret's golden fried chicken, or just a plain old warm biscuit with a ribbon of sorghum stitched across its top.

He stopped once at a sheep ranch where the owner gave Bigger a hard look. "Don't know if I can do much for you, sonny," the man growled. "That dog you got there—why, he looks like a sheep killer to me. If I were to put you up, and he were to so much as muss the wool on one a my flock—I'd be obliged to shoot him, skin him, and nail his pesky hide to this here door!"

"Nossir, I don't think he's a sheep killer," Tyler answered, but the possibility that Bigger, being hungry, might make a meal out of an unwary lamb worried him. "I'll see to it he sleeps right beside me all night," he promised.

Later, in a lean-to behind the house where the rancher offered him a place to sleep, Tyler tied the rope from his bedroll around Bigger's neck and the other end around his own ankle. "Wish folks weren't always threatening to send you to perdition!" he complained. "Last thing I need is to lose you." Bigger settled himself against Tyler's thigh as if to say he held no grudges about their peculiar new sleeping arrangements.

* * *

94

Even after he went deeper into the desert, in village after village, with stranger after stranger, the information about General Shelby didn't change. Frowns and curious glances were followed by, "No, haven't seen anything like what you're describin', son. No men, no soldiers, nothin'. War's over, y'know; those Union boys made their point. Ain't no more soldiering to be done."

Sometimes Tyler took a meal with folks he couldn't talk to. He couldn't understand their language, and they couldn't understand his. The mothers in those small clay homes, their eyes soft and mild in their smooth, brown faces, gave him cornmeal cakes with beans on top, and once he drank goat's milk which tasted richer even than Calico's cream.

In the beginning Tyler had been curious about Bigger's past, about what made the dog flinch so readily, what made him curl his lip so often. None of that mattered anymore. What counted was that Bigger was a sticktight, the name Mama gave to the burrs that used to get snagged in Maggie's ears and tail. Whenever he spoke to Bigger, he always said *we*. "*We* will do this, Bigger," he'd say, or, "*We'll* go that way, Bigger." In the dog's one blue eye and one brown eye there was a comforting reply: *Yes, that suits me,* and, *Go where you need to go; I'll stick tight.*

Finally, tired as he was, Tyler went back to reading Papa's letters. No matter how often he did (the paper seemed to grow thinner and more transparent each evening because the pages had been handled so often), he discovered something new in the words.

"Dear Family:

If I should die in this war, I want you all to stay where you are. Sweet Creek is as good a home place as any man could've picked in this whole wide world. If need be, Tyler can learn to run things."

Yes, Papa, I already have, Tyler wanted to tell him.

"The thing is to hold fast to each other."

Yes, Papa, that's what we've done for four long years, Tyler whispered.

"That oldest boy of mine, being the good son he is, can teach little Lucas what he needs to know."

I'm trying to, Papa.

"And, Wife, I know you will raise up our Rosa Lee to be as fine a woman as her mother."

Rosa Lee helps Mama make butter now, Papa; you'd be proud of her.

After a while there were no more villages on the plains, only small ranches scattered so far apart that sometimes Tyler walked for days without seeing a soul. There were no roads through the sagebrush. He simply followed dim trails through the sun-scorched grass that had been made by antelope and rabbits and coyotes.

Sometimes Tyler roasted a lizard for supper after he'd knocked one senseless as it sunned itself in the heat of the day. The desert rabbits were too fleet-footed for Bigger to run down anymore because he, too, was so thin his sides had caved in under his thick fur. Tyler learned how to slice cacti and squeeze moisture out of the pieces. With the prickles removed, the flesh of certain cacti tasted sweet, almost like a piece of fruit. Bigger relished such treats, too.

One night, a terrible thunderstorm boomed across the prairie. Lightning made the sky bright as day, and the dry gully Tyler had camped beside overran its banks. He scooped up his gear, and raced for higher ground; somehow Uncle Matt's blue kerchief was carried away by the rushing water.

It was late afternoon when Tyler spotted General Shelby's troops. He disbelieved what he saw. He turned his gaze away.

He looked again. A long line of men, riding in twos and threes, were etched against the distant horizon. Heat shimmered off the baked, brown land in quivering sheets. Should he take those black figures, no larger than ants against the skyline, to be what he'd been searching for? Tyler squinted hard; perhaps he was looking at a mirage.

"Bigger," he whispered, finally willing to accept what was there, "I think maybe it's General Shelby and his men!" But they were miles away. Can I catch up to them before they recede even farther into the distance? Tyler wondered. Oh, what he'd give for a horse, even a sorry, crippled-up glass-eyed old has-been like the one Mr. Blackburn rode to school!

Tyler walked faster, finally forced himself into a trot. Bigger loped along behind. "You got four legs instead of only two," Tyler complained, panting. He couldn't keep up such a pace; neither could Bigger. They didn't have the kind of strength they'd had when their journey started. Tyler's breath rattled in his chest; sweat soaked his clothes till he looked as if he'd been standing in a rain. He longed to quench his thirst but knew he shouldn't drink until he found a place to refill his canteen.

"So many men riding together are bound to leave a trail that's easy to follow," he told Bigger when they both dropped back to a walk. "Even if we don't catch 'em today we'll be able to track 'em pretty easy tomorrow and the day after."

And then—oh then—Papa would clap him against his hard chest, would cry, "Tyler! Tyler! Is it really you, boy?" His smile would be wide and welcoming. In a few days he and Papa could turn around and go home. *Home.* The word was as beautiful as the pale blue aggie in his pocket, and he rolled it on his tongue: *Home, home.* The word was round, smooth, complete.

Tyler caught up with the soldiers after they'd pitched camp on the banks of the Rio Grande. He was surprised: He'd expected General Shelby's men would be in rank, that their uniforms would be a credit to them, that they would look purposeful and military.

Instead, some were dressed in raggedy castoffs (taken from dead men on some battlefield? Tyler asked himself), and a few were bareheaded, their foreheads and noses blistered from the desert sun, their lips cracked and bleeding. Their eyes glittered deep in their sockets, their cheeks were drawn, their horses looked badly fed.

As quickly as he could Tyler scanned the knots of men

for a glimpse of Black Jack Bohannon. Papa was so tall he'd stand out anywhere. His hair and beard were so black he'd look like no one else. His voice would be richer than any other soldier's, his laugh would be merrier.

Nowhere, though, could he see a man who looked like Papa.

"Hey, there, sonny—you drop down on us out of the sky or what?" a voice behind him asked roughly. The man Tyler turned to face had a pair of eyes so bloodshot they almost matched his dirty red hair.

"Came from Missouri," Tyler said, and felt his shoulders sag with disappointment. Clayton had been right, after all; Papa didn't want to be found. Maybe Papa saw him coming and had gone off to hide.

"You've traveled a long ways," the man admitted. "Guess the next question is *why?*"

"I came looking for my pa," Tyler mumbled, suddenly too tired to stand anymore. He lowered himself to the ground, and draped his arms loosely around his knees. Bigger collapsed beside him. The soldier crouched next to them, peering curiously first at Tyler, then at Bigger.

"What makes you think your pa's here?" he asked.

"I figured he threw in with General Shelby," Tyler whispered. "Someone back there"—he jerked his thumb wearily in the direction he'd come from—"told me Shelby was going to leave the country, that he was headed for Mexico. We hadn't heard from Papa in a good long while, so I got to thinking maybe he'd decided to—"

"You're on target so far," the soldier admitted. "Most of these boys are from Shelby's outfit, sure enough, about five, six hundred chaps in all. 'Course, a few came over to us from other divisions, men no more anxious to live under the heel of Federal boots than Shelby. Now, son, what would your pa's name be?"

"John Bohannon. Folks back home call him Black Jack."

"Well, ain't you in luck! Black Jack's here, all right. He's a favorite with the boys, even though he's rougher'n a cob on 'em sometimes. Doesn't have much time for spinnin' yarns or playin' the fool. Not him!"

No time for yarns or foolery? But that's what Papa was famous for all up and down Sweet Creek. . . .

"Matter of fact, I saw him earlier today," the soldier went on. "Lemme say you got here just in time, son. If you'd arrived a couple of days later you'd have missed us altogether. Your informant was right—we plan to cross over into Mexico in the morning."

This was the moment he'd waited for. Papa was here. It was the reason he and Bigger had traveled more than eight hundred miles together, why he'd worn out one pair of shoes and was now wearing a dead man's. The moment had arrived—but Tyler was too exhausted to savor it.

"Can you point him out to me?" he asked his red-eyed companion. "For sure he won't know *me* because he's been gone from home four years and I've growed up a lot since he went away." Of course he'd know Papa anywhere—wouldn't he? The fact that he might not had never occurred to Tyler.

"You don't have long to wait," the stranger said. "There he goes now, him on that slat-sided gray horse." Tyler followed the pointing finger with hungry eyes.

The gray horse was sharp-shouldered and high in the

100

croup; its ribs showed through its hide like staves on a barrel. But Papa had ridden away on Ransom, a tall, red horse with haunches as powerful as a bull's, a horse that turned the color of bronze in the sun. He'd come by his name because Papa once said he was worth a king's ransom. Had proud Ransom fallen somewhere in the war?

Tyler got quickly to his feet, galvanized by the sight of the man he'd come so far to find. He hurried forward, and when he got closer he called softly, "Papa! Papa, it's me!"

The rider reined in his gray horse and turned sharply. Tyler felt himself pull back. The man who stared down at him looked nothing like the person he'd been seeking. The rider's eyes burned like hot coals in his head, not with the cheery, sassy glow that Tyler remembered. This man's black beard was shot with strands of gray; his cheeks, once so ruddy and full, were hollowed out. The mouth beneath the thick, gray-streaked mustache was a savage, narrow line. The stranger didn't smile.

"Who are you to call me Papa, young feller?" he demanded, a frown deepening the creases on his forehead.

"It's me, Papa," Tyler said. "It's me, Tyler, come all the way from Sweet Creek to find you."

"Tyler?" Black Jack Bohannon repeated the name with doubt, then with astonishment. "Tyler? Come down from Missouri? *That* Tyler?"

"That Tyler," the boy said, his heart as tender and swollen as it had been in all his dreams. No sooner did he reach out to touch the rider's leg than Black Jack climbed down off his gray horse. His eyes, too, were bloodshot, and Tyler could see the brim of his hat was blackened with sweat and dirt, his shirt collar ragged and filthy.

101

"Why, son, you look considerable different than when I left home," Black Jack said, his voice gone soft with amazement. "Thinner'n a peeled willow switch, ain't you, and a lot taller than I remember!" He glanced down at Bigger. "That your dog?" he wanted to know. "You had to get another'n because something happened to that nice little Maggie-dog who used to hunt squirrels with me?"

"Maggie's fine, got a new batch of pups, four of 'em," Tyler answered. "This here dog"—he turned to look at Bigger himself—"this dog just sort of hitched up with me, and we decided to travel together permanently."

Black Jack laid his hand on Tyler's shoulder, a sudden flash of alarm showing in his red-rimmed black eyes. "Has something happened back there on the creek?" he demanded. "Your Mama—Rosa Lee—are they—?"

"They were fine when I left them, Papa," Tyler said. "Lucas too. What I came for was to bring you home. We've been waiting so long, and I figured maybe you didn't know how much we—"

Black Jack massaged Tyler's shoulder with strong, hard fingers before he turned aside. "We'll talk about it later, son." He pointed down the bank to the river, his voice not soft anymore but hard and eager. "See there, Ty? We'll finish lashing those skiffs together by nightfall. The plan is to clamber aboard and swim the horses and mules across tomorrow if rains upstream haven't made the water too deep or set it flowing too fast."

"But, Papa—"

"Later, son. There'll be time for talk tomorrow. Right now I'd better get myself down there and help my boys along. You wait for me here." He swung onto his thin

102

gray horse and Tyler watched Black Jack hurry down to the edge of the river.

My boys, Papa had called the men who worked below. Tyler rubbed the back of his blistered neck, tried to pull his shirt collar higher. Absentmindedly, he stroked Bigger's head. He'd found Papa, exactly as he'd vowed to do. Somehow, though, nothing was exactly like he'd dreamed it would be. Was he different now, or was Papa?

★ 12 ★

THAT NIGHT, AROUND MESQUITE FIRES SCATTERED LIKE bright islands up and down the riverbank, the men of the Iron Cavalry Brigade talked of Mexico. Several antelope had been killed earlier in the day; the cool desert air was fragrant with the smell of roasting meat. In the slow-moving river below, Texas stars were reflected like silver coins tossed onto the black water.

"A year, not much more, and we'll be ready to head back this way," one soldier chortled, wiping scarlet meat juices from his chin with the back of his hand. "Those Yankees think the war ended just because General Lee held up a white flag at Appomattox? Well, think again, boys—*we* got other plans!"

"You tell 'em, Rowdy!" someone hollered back. "And won't it be a surprise to 'em when we come riding hell-for-leather over this border again some fine day!"

"We need to keep recruitin', though," another voice warned. "We need an *army*, not just a bunch of fellers with dreams of secession still burnin' in their brains."

Tyler listened. No man talked of home. Instead, all

eyes were turned toward Mexico. He shot a look at Papa. In the firelight, Black Jack's eyes were narrow and reflective. It was impossible to tell exactly what he was thinking. Papa had promised they would talk, but now he chewed his ration of charred antelope meat, preoccupied with matters Tyler could only guess at.

Later, when the soldiers bedded down for the night, Tyler lay side by side with Papa. Overhead, the points of the stars had become as sharp as knives. Down the riverbank someone played a harmonica softly. In the distance a coyote howled. Tyler was tempted to reach out to touch Black Jack and whisper, "About going home, Papa. No need for us to hurry. You can rest here as long as you need to." But he stayed his hand.

He studied the arch of his father's shoulder carved blackly against the dying firelight. He's tired, Tyler reminded himself, that's why he's so quiet. After all, he'd watched Papa work all afternoon building skiffs, had tried to be of help himself, had seen the sweat stand out on Papa's forehead like rows of glass beads. It would be unkind to pester him tonight, Tyler decided; it would be best to wait.

When they were finally alone together, though, after everyone else had crossed the Rio Grande, they'd have the pleasure of getting acquainted again. Maybe Papa would remark in greater detail about how much he'd grown, how tall he'd gotten in the past four years. Tyler smiled in the dark.

As they headed back to Sweet Creek, Papa no doubt would tell him stories about the war, how glad he was it was over, how good it would be to be home again. Tyler savored the soon-to-come moments they would share, then touched his father so lightly on the shoulder that Black Jack never stirred.

No matter what anyone said, I knew you were still alive, Tyler told the arched black shoulder. I knew I could find you if I tried hard enough, Papa. Against his other flank, he felt Bigger's warm body; he reached out to bury his fingers in the dog's thick coat. For the first time since he left Sweet Creek, Tyler was happy.

The men of the Iron Brigade were up before dawn embroidered itself like a thin green ribbon on the black skyline. Coffee was brewed, and the soldiers ate hardtack and cold, roasted meat as they paced back and forth, wolfing their grub down as greedily as Bigger did when he was really hungry, which lately was all the time. A few men had already begun to load the skiffs with saddles, bedrolls, barrels.

Before long the first skiff was ready to be pushed off the riverbank to test how the water was running. A dozen men boarded it, and with long poles began to push their way across to the other side as the rising sun briefly turned the Rio Grande into a river of blood. The current was sluggish, which meant crossing would be fairly safe, and soon another skiff was loaded. A few mules were roped together and swam across behind it.

"It's goin' to work fine," Tyler heard Papa call out. "The rest of you boys, soon as those skiffs are poled back here, get ready to load 'em up again. Let's be quick about this; we ain't come all this way to let Phil Sheridan and his blue boys put us in irons at the last minute!"

A moment later Papa peeled off his hat as a man on a red horse came riding along the bank. "Ah, here comes Jo

106

Shelby," he said, tapping Tyler on the shoulder. "Wonder what he's got on his mind today?"

In a moment it was clear what the general planned to do. He ordered the battle flag of the Iron Brigade spread on the ground at his horse's feet. Tyler watched as General Shelby plucked the black plume from his hatband and threw it onto the Stars and Bars. Two men came forward carrying a large stone, which they laid on the flag along with the general's feather. All four corners were wrapped around the stone, then flag, stone, and plume were pitched into the river. A bugler played taps. The rock sank quickly while edges of the flag fluttered up, then it too vanished beneath the dark water.

A glad hurrah went up from everyone on the bank. "Ho, for Mexico!" someone cried. "Louder, boys—ho, for Mexico!" Papa raised his hat in the air, too, and Tyler saw Black Jack's hair was as matted and gray-streaked as his beard. "God bless us all!" he yelled.

As soon as the first skiffs returned, more loading was done—sacks of flour, sugar, rice, coffee; boxes of Enfield rifles and ammunition; three barrels of whiskey. Tyler fell to work beside Papa. Perhaps this would be a good time to discuss a few of the things that were on his mind.

"We waited to hear after the war was over, Papa," he explained, "then I figured maybe you'd got shot and might be needing help. That's when I decided to—"

"I did get shot, son," Papa announced gruffly. Tyler stared. In his letters Papa never mentioned being wounded. "Was lucky, though, not like some a those poor lads I saw. Boys not much older than you, Ty, their arms, legs, faces blasted away. All I took was a bullet in the fleshy part of my leg," he admitted, pointing at his thigh.

"If I'd taken it in the bone, though, I'd likely have died on the spot, if not from the wound then from the amputation I'd have had," he went on. "It's an awful thing to watch a man get his leg sawed off with tools that ain't clean, no anesthetic to ease his pain, no proper bandages to wrap up his wound. But it was done, Ty, and I'll hear those boys' screams in my ears till I go to my grave."

"You never mentioned such things in your letters, Papa," Tyler murmured, remembering what he'd read about playing baseball, about the woods with a stream running through it, the good pasture for the horses that was nearby.

"Some tales are too awful to be told, son," Black Jack said, and in his father's eyes Tyler saw a reflection of events that couldn't now be unseen or unremembered. It was the same look that had been in graybeard's eyes and in the eyes of the stranger at Sweet Creek.

"Harold Crowe from over on Pepper Creek—you know him, don't you, Papa?—well, he got blinded in one eye," Tyler spoke up quickly, glad at least that Papa was finally talking. "I figured I'd better come to find you in case such a thing had happened to you. But when we get back home . . ."

Just then, down near the edge of the water, one of the horses began to buck and pitch, interrupting Tyler in midsentence. With white, rolling eyes it tried to turn back from the river and scramble up the bank to freedom.

"Get that darn fool into the water where he belongs!" Papa yelled, leaping forward and waving both arms. "We can't afford to lose a single one a those horses, boys!" At the sight of Papa, the animal turned, plunged obediently

108

into the river, and began to swim hard for the distant shore.

"When we get back home," Tyler began, intending to take up the conversation where it had been interrupted, "you'll be mighty glad to see how good the place looks. Calico had a fine heifer calf this spring, and the garden looks like it'll be our best one ever." He smiled at Papa, remembering how fine he'd left things back there. "Rosa Lee claims she can't remember you, but as soon as you're home, why she'll—"

"Easy now, son," Papa warned, and held up a hand. "There's a lot for me to do before I can ever come home again."

Tyler was silent a moment. "But the war's over, Papa," he whispered. "Mr. Lincoln's dead. They got Jeff Davis in irons over there at Fortress Monroe. I heard talk about the new president, Andy Johnson, giving amnesty to the Confederates, so folks'll be able to take up where they left off before the war came along. We can all—"

"There'll be no takin' up anything for me, Ty. It ain't right what the Union did to us," Papa insisted. "We've got a debt to settle with 'em, son, and Jo Shelby's the man to show us how to do it. I can't go home now, not till we've evened the score."

"But, Papa, I came so far . . ." Tyler couldn't believe how small and faraway his voice sounded. "I finally found you. Mama and Lucas are waiting—even Rosa Lee—can't we—?"

"Son, sometimes a man gets to a certain place because that's where his road leads him." Behind Papa's brooding black eyes was a pain that made Tyler hold his own tongue. "Only a man don't know exactly where that road's

109

takin' him, not till he gets to the end of it," Papa explained. "I never meant to be away so long, Ty, but the truth is, the road I'm travelin' on ain't come to an end yet." He reached out to lay a hand on Tyler's shoulder.

"You're a sensible, steady fellow, like your Uncle Matthew," he went on. "You don't understand, just like he didn't. He called me a fool when I volunteered, told me I ought to have better sense. It was a young man's war, he said. Ty, it was *my* war, and I ain't ready to quit fightin' it, not by a long shot!"

Black Jack loaded his saddle and gear onto the last skiff going across the river. He whacked his sad-looking gray horse on the rump and the animal leaped forward into the water. Tyler looked straight into Papa's face, trying to fix forever in his mind those somber eyes, those hollow cheeks, that savage mouth beneath a mustache that no longer was the color of a beaver's coat.

Tyler remembered the kiss he'd planted on Lucas's eyebrow. You couldn't kiss your father, though, not in front of a bunch of soldiers, even if it was the last time in this world you might ever see him.

I came so far, Tyler thought. So far. Only to lose Papa again. How could he make sure Papa would never forget him? That no matter how far from Sweet Creek Black Jack Bohannon traveled he'd always remember there was a boy at home named Tyler?

Tyler reached in his pocket. He took out the pale, blue-white aggie. It lay warm and smooth in his hand.

"Here, Papa. Take this. You gave it to me a long time ago, remember? You told me it was a good-luck piece. Everybody needs as much of that as they can get, you said. I want you to have it now, Papa."

Black Jack plucked the marble out of Tyler's palm. "Why, son! You've kept it all these years." He smiled one of his rare, old, cheery smiles. "I'll make you a bargain, Ty. I'll keep it with me till we meet again, then you can have it back. Shall we shake on it?"

Tyler held out his hand. Papa's grip was firm and determined. "Take care, son," he counseled gently. Tyler was sure there was affection, maybe even love, in his father's glance. "You're a good boy, fine as they make 'em, and I'm right proud you're mine. When this is all over— and if I live through it—I'll come up our road and cross that bridge over Sweet Creek. Then we'll be together again. But I can't quit now, Ty, not until things get put back the way they were before them Union boys turned it all upside down for us."

Before Tyler could say good-bye, Black Jack turned and leaped onto the skiff. With a glad cry, six or seven men jumped on behind him. The boy realized there was time enough before Papa pushed off from the riverbank that he could make the leap himself.

Yes, I could, Tyler thought. He could cross over into Mexico, could learn to shoot a rifle as well as Papa, could fight right beside him when the Iron Brigade of Missouri finally came back to settle the score with the Union.

Bigger could go, too. It would be a grand adventure, one such as few boys would ever be lucky enough to have. Cousin Clayton would never get over being pea-green jealous! Was there any law that said he had to go back to Sweet Creek? No, there wasn't. Lucas could take over for him at home, just as *he'd* taken over for Papa.

Tyler stood rooted on the bank as the men on Papa's skiff shoved off and began to pole across the Rio Grande.

On the opposite shore, soldiers were tearing the other rafts apart and packing up the wood to be used later for fires in a country where firewood was sure to be scarce. Black Jack's skiff was the last to land. The men he'd gone over with pulled the craft onto the bank and began to dismantle it too.

Tyler watched as long as he could, saw Papa saddle his slat-sided gray horse and mount up. He waved a long time but Papa must not have seen because he didn't wave back. The men who'd come aground earlier had already moved out, had once again become black dots crawling along the horizon. Black Jack followed them, dust rising like plumes around his horse's hooves.

Tyler watched until the bleak horizon was emptied of men and mules and horses. His heart felt battered and sore. He pressed both hands hard against his breastbone to subdue the pain he felt inside. He couldn't let his heart break. Not now. Not yet.

On his side of the river, a hot, dry wind whispered through the scrubby grass. Overhead, a pair of buzzards wheeled slowly against the hard, blue Texas sky. Below, the brown Rio Grande flowed inexorably to the sea.

Tyler squatted beside Bigger. The dog seemed to be waiting to hear a closure to the long adventure they'd shared. I've told Bigger so much about Papa, Tyler mused, about what life would be like when we all got home.

What should I tell him now? the boy asked himself. He didn't want to admit what he knew was true. He wanted to hold it off as long as he could. Something in Bigger's patient, two-colored glance, though, finally let him put into words a decision that would change the rest of his life while letting it remain forever the same.

"Dreams are funny things, Bigger," Tyler said, staring across the river. "The one Papa's got is different from mine. He can't let go of it. No matter how much it costs, Papa will hang on to that dream he's got in his head." The dog listened, his shoulder pressed against the boy's knee, his brown eye warm, his blue eye cool. Tyler looped an arm around Bigger's neck.

"But you know what, Bigger?" Bigger waited. Tyler swallowed hard. His heart was bruised; his eyes burned. "I think it's time for me to turn loose of mine."

☆ 13 ☆

GOING HOME, THE JOURNEY ACROSS TEXAS WENT FASTER because this time Tyler knew exactly where he was headed.

In the hill country the creeks once again became good for fishing. The shade beneath the oaks and maples, a few beginning to change color, was cool and dark. The rocky hills of Arkansas were a welcome sight but nothing compared to how Tyler felt when he crossed the border into Missouri. Soon he recognized parts of the country he'd passed through before. At last he realized he was no more than two weeks from home.

He'd read Papa's letters often on the trip to the banks of the Rio Grande, but now he read them every night. Somehow, he had to make sense of what had happened, to come to terms with the fact he'd likely never see Black Jack Bohannon again.

Certain phrases, Tyler knew, would live in his heart forever. "Size don't make a man a hero; it's his heart that accounts for that. . . . If I should die in this war, I want you all to stay where you are . . . hold fast to each other

114

... Tyler, being the good son he is, can teach little Lucas what he needs to know. . . ."

Yes, Lucas and Rosa Lee, with their hot, dark looks just like Papa's, might need a steady hand. "But it's going to be hard to tell them, Mama especially, that Papa's not coming home," he confessed to Bigger.

How should I break the news to them? he wondered. "Are there special words I should use, Bigger, ones that will make it easier for them to understand?"

The answer in Bigger's eyes was the one he already knew: *You have to tell them the truth.* That Papa said the war was *his* war, that he'd stick it out no matter how long it took, that the score with the Union had to be settled.

Tyler flinched at what the task would be like. It wouldn't be so hard on Rosa Lee, but Lucas had been so sure life would be right again; now he'd bear the pain of knowing it never would. And when Mama knew the truth, oh, the look that would come into her summer-blue eyes!

A week later, when Tyler realized he was within fifty miles of New Hope, he knew he had a choice to make: to stop—or not to stop—at Uncle Matt's. He could plainly imagine what would take place when he showed up, alone, at Riley's Farm and Home Store.

"Nyah!—I told ya your papa didn't want to be found!" Clayton would crow. Tyler gritted his teeth to think of the self-satisfied shine in Clayton's mean little eyes.

Uncle Matt wouldn't be rude, of course. Just the same, a regretful expression would make his pale storekeeper's face seem more mournful than ever. Aunt Margaret would cluck to herself, "Poor Ellen! Three young ones to raise all alone, a widow just as surely as if her husband was dead and buried!" Mama would choke on that kind of pity.

"Can't go to New Hope yet," Tyler admitted to Bigger with a sigh, eager to put off a visit until he'd thoroughly collected his wits. "I'll wait till I've been home a while before I go tell Uncle Matt what happened. Then I'll give him back the money I haven't spent." The only purchase he'd made had been the canteen, meat, and biscuits somewhere in Texas; Uncle Matt would have no need to regret his investment.

"Clayton will be a pain, Bigger, but by that time maybe I'll know more about what I think myself and can work up some sassy answers for him," Tyler promised himself, laying a hand on Bigger's wide head.

Ah, Bigger! What would he have done without Bigger? "Uncle Matt was crazy to even think about shooting you!" he exclaimed. "Why, traveling with you made everything possible. Without you, well . . ." The truth was, Tyler couldn't imagine Isaac or Pea Ridge or descending that ladder of rivers toward Eagle Pass without Bigger. Without Bigger his heart surely would have broken as he watched Papa disappear, probably forever, into Mexico.

The next morning Tyler made a wide detour around New Hope, which brought him close to the smaller village of McMinnville to the west. He fingered the money he'd carried for almost four months in his pocket.

There was a store in McMinnville, he remembered. It would be nice to take something back to the three who were waiting on Sweet Creek. He couldn't bring Papa home but he could surely get some ribbons for Rosa Lee, an apron for Mama, a good knife for Lucas. Later he'd thank Uncle Matt for the money, would tell him what he'd spent part of it on, would promise to pay it all back when he could.

McMinnville wasn't as big as Lucas recalled, and the store in the middle of town was a smaller version of Uncle Matt's. He hurried down the street toward it, aware of the curious glances he got from a few townsfolk as they went about their usual business.

"Hey, sonny!"

The voice that called out to him from the alley beside the store was harsh. Tyler turned, startled, to face whoever had spoken. The man who came toward him was huge. His hair was a mixture of tangled, dirty copper and yellow wires; his eyes beneath a pair of beetling brows were so tiny it was impossible to tell what color they were.

"Where'd you get that dog, sonny?" the man demanded.

"Bigger? Why, he's just a . . ." Tyler began, intending to explain how the dog had been abandoned by its master, then tied in Uncle Matt's yard. He was about to go on when he saw that the hackles on Bigger's neck were stiff. The dog's upper lip was curled back from his teeth. Tyler had been so sure Bigger had mostly gotten over his old ways, but now his pale blue eye was filled with cold fury, and a hot blaze burned in the brown one.

Tyler couldn't decide which was more alarming, the bearish man who blocked the street in front of him, or the change that had suddenly come over Bigger. The dog seemed to have become once again what Uncle Matt had predicted he was: a devil.

"We've been t-t-t-traveling together," Tyler stammered, "and n-n-n-now I'm headed for home."

"There ain't goin' to be no more together about it,

sonny," the man boomed. "That's *my* dog and I aim to take him back. Right now!" He took a step forward, his heavy boots raising mushrooms of dust in the street.

"What do you mean, *your* dog?" Tyler said, amazed by the unexpected hard edge in his own voice. Had he traveled all the way to Texas and back to be pushed around now? Nope. He laid his hand possessively on Bigger's neck. "This here dog's a stray. Don't belong to nobody."

"Stray my hind end. That dog's mine, belonged to me for more'n three years. Had t'give him up temporarily when I headed outa New Hope in a hurry. But now I'm back—and I aim to take *him* back."

"Wait!" Tyler cried. Uncle Matt's money was a welcome wad in his pocket. His uncle's final words had been *If you spend it all, that's fine by me. That's what I meant it for.* "I'll buy him off you!"

"Buy 'im? What if I don't want to sell 'im?" the man sneered.

"I don't have a dog," Tyler lied, "and since him and me been traveling together for quite a while, well, I'd like to buy him if you're willing to sell him."

"Well, I ain't. That mutt is the best watchdog I ever owned. He'd as soon take the leg off a man as look at 'im. I got 'im as a pup, see, and made sure he grew up to have a temper hotter'n a banked fire. Made that pooch mean by tormentin' him, because that's exactly how I wanted him to be." He raised his brows as if a surprising thought had just occurred to him. "Come to think of it, how'd *you* make up to 'im without gettin' turned into mincemeat?"

Bigger finally made up to me, Tyler wanted to explain, it wasn't me making up to him. It all made sense now. Bigger flinching every time a hand was held out . . .

118

Bigger curling his lip at Isaac . . . Bigger snarling at the shovel the gravedigger had raised . . . always imagining he was going to get beat on again.

Now the important thing was just to own Bigger fair and square. Tyler dug into his pocket and brought out the paper money Uncle Matt had given him. "There's ten dollars here," he said. "Count it if you want. I'm willing to pay that much."

The man took the bills, counted them, and smiled. "Well, sonny, that's right decent of you! I can always use ten dollars. Fact is, though, I can't let go a that dog."

"But you took my money!" Tyler objected. "So the dog's mine. A deal is a deal."

The man snickered, his eyes no bigger than raisins under his brows. "No, sonny, you don't unnerstan'. You and me got no deal. This here money is what I'm goin' to have to charge you for runnin' off with my dog without permission." The man stripped his belt off, then swaggered toward Bigger. "C'mere, you stupid mutt, lemme put this here around your—"

Bigger didn't make a sound. He launched himself out of the street, straight into the man's face. His lips were curled back so fiercely that the top of his nose was deeply ridged, like dried ruts in a road after a rain. Tyler heard a snarl build deep inside the dog. It was the voice of the devil himself. Bigger caught his former master across the face with bared teeth, and left a long row of marks that instantly began to bleed.

The man toppled backward into the street, the paper bills fluttering to the ground around him. People began to gather, and Tyler hoped someone would offer to do something. Then he saw the man lift himself to his knees.

He reached for the pistol in a small holster tied to his boot.

"No!" Tyler hollered. "Wait! I got more money! Here, I'll give it all to—" He dug frantically in his pocket for the coins he knew were still there. "Looka here, mister—you can have everything!"

The man raised his pistol. Bigger vaulted into the air a second time, moving like a live bullet himself, his devil voice loud enough to make the bystanders in the street cover their ears. Tyler saw a gleam of revenge in Bigger's blue-and-brown gaze; the dog's white bib was like a silver shield in the noontime glare.

When the shot rang out, Bigger's devil shriek went silent in midair. A new sound came out of his barrel chest, soft and gurgling, like spring water welling out of the ground. He fell into the dust like a piece of clothing, an old coat that someone had dropped off a passing wagon. He raised his head, and tried to get to his feet again.

The man, snorting hard, steadied his pistol for a second shot. Tyler launched himself against the pointing arm and knocked the weapon aside. "Why, you sassy, no good little brat!" the man yelled, and raised his fist like a club. "I'll teach you—"

"You ain't goin' to teach him anything, mister," barked a tall man who came loping across the street. He didn't wear a badge but folks cleared a path for him. "And I'll take this gun while I'm at it," he snapped, scooping the pistol out of the dust. "It's a misdemeanor to discharge firearms within the city limits of McMinnville—didn't you read the sign posted down the road a ways?"

Someone gathered up the money and handed it to

Tyler. He stuffed it in his pocket without looking at it, then knelt at Bigger's side.

In the center of the dog's white bib there was a small, dainty red flower that slowly began to bloom. Bigger's eyes were open. "Bigger?" Tyler called urgently. "Hang on, Bigger! We're almost there. Hang on, boy!—I'll get something to carry you on—we'll both be home soon. Maggie's pups will—"

As he watched, Bigger's warm brown eye lost its fiery glow. The blue eye became cooler and more mysterious than ever. Tyler bent his face close to the dog's ear. There was something he had to say.

"Good-bye, Bigger," he whispered, sure the dog could still hear. Bigger's fur was warm against his cheek. There'd been no time to say good-bye to Papa, so this farewell was even more important.

"Good-bye, Bigger," he called again. "Good-bye, good-bye." This time, Tyler didn't press his hands against his chest to dull the pain he felt inside. This time, he let his heart break.

A man from the tannery across the street fixed a sling between two poles. He helped Tyler lay Bigger on it, even secured the dog's slowly stiffening body to it so he wouldn't slide off as the travois was dragged along.

"My advice, son, is to bury 'im here and now. Weather's still fearsome hot; he'll bloat up on you like a dead hog. The smell will make you hold your nose all the way to where you're goin'. I got a place out back if you want to dig a—"

"I don't," Tyler answered curtly. He knew exactly where he wanted to bury Bigger, and it definitely was not in back of somebody's tanyard in McMinnville. "This is where he got killed," Tyler muttered, "but he sure don't have to spend all eternity here."

"Suit yourself, sonny," the tanner murmured, stepping aside, "but I guarantee you he'll turn out to be a mighty fragrant companion."

Tyler knew what the man had said about the heat was true, so he traveled toward home under the stars and a moon that was as narrow as one of Lucas's eyebrows. The next day he slept in the deepest shade he could find, first covering Bigger's body with leaves and branches soaked in creek water to keep it cool.

It was evening when he came to the three apple trees on the ridge overlooking the bridge across Sweet Creek. Their white blooms were gone now; in their place were apples the size of Rosa Lee's fist. Every spring, those trees would once again look like three sisters in pale dresses on their way to church. Could there be a better place for Bigger to rest?

The earth beneath the trees was soft and loamy. Tyler dug first with his knife, then with his bare hands. He worked until he had scooped a place deep enough for Bigger to lie, then be covered over with enough dirt so that foxes or badgers wouldn't dig him up again and feast on his bones.

Tyler stroked Bigger's wide head and pressed his eyes closed, first the blue one, now cloudy in death, then the brown one, its fire long gone. Bigger's coat still felt soft, was still as thick as a bear cub's. Tyler wrapped the canvas sling around the dog and lowered him into the grave.

Before he covered him over with dirt, he talked to Bigger one last time.

"Bigger, if there'd been any way I could've saved you . . ." Tyler reviewed again in his mind the scene in McMinnville: the man with raisin eyes; the pistol; the dainty red flower pinned to Bigger's white bib. "But there was nothing I could do, Bigger," he apologized.

"Mostly, though, I regret what that man did to you before I ever knew you." As Tyler talked, the bruise in his heart was eased. "Making you mean, tormenting you like he did, so's Uncle Matt would claim a devil lived inside you. I never would've done that to you, Bigger. You know that, don't you?" There was no reply, but Tyler imagined the look in Bigger's eyes if an answer had been possible.

No, you never would have, his cool blue eye would have agreed.

No way under the sun or the moon, the warm brown eye would have declared.

Tyler scooped handfuls of dirt over the canvas. He smoothed the earth on top and pressed it down. In the spring, new grass as fine as a baby's hair would cover this mound. Petals from the apple trees would fall here like snow; every time he passed this way he'd be able to look up and know Bigger had come home, too.

Tyler walked down the slope. He looked back once. The three trees were silhouetted against the evening sky; at their feet, he could barely make out the fresh, dark oval in the earth. He turned, and crossed the bridge over Sweet Creek, his footsteps echoing softly on the night air. A half-mile later, he could see Mama had lit the lamp in the kitchen.

123

He waited a while before going through the gate. Lucas must've fixed the latch because it wasn't loose anymore. Inside the house Maggie gave a warning bark, hearing what she took to be a stranger in the road. Mama opened the door, and Maggie rushed out. She came forward with a second warning bark, but by the time she reached the gate she was wiggly with glee.

He was home. The word was round, smooth, complete.

☆14☆

ROSA LEE GRABBED HER RIBBONS AND WANTED THEM ALL tied in her hair at once. "Look, Mama—blue and green and red and yellow!" she cried.

Mama smoothed her new apron with reddened fingers. "Why, son, this is so pretty I'll save it for Sundays," she promised. Lucas opened and closed his knife so often Tyler finally warned him with a smile, "Careful, Lucas, or you'll wear that out before you've even had a chance to use it." How glad he was he'd taken the time—even as Bigger lay in the tanyard—to make the purchases that now pleased Rosa Lee and Mama and Lucas so much.

Of course, they all wanted to know if he'd found Papa.

"I did, for certain," Tyler reported. Their eyes glowed in the lamplight, but on his first night home it seemed best to tell them only the parts of the story that would be easiest for them to digest.

"Papa's different now," he explained. "Remember what the war did to Oat Snepp's brother? To Mr. Harold Crowe? Well, war does different things to different people. The truth is, it's lit a fire in Papa that water can't put out." Mama nodded; Tyler knew she understood exactly what he meant.

"A fire?" Rosa Lee echoed. "Papa caught on fire?"

Lucas was quiet for a moment. "Will he ever come home, Ty?" he asked finally, anguish showing in his eyes. Being a second son, he missed Papa in his own special way.

"Well, it's hard to tell for sure about things like that, Lucas," Tyler answered. There'd be other times he and Lucas could discuss this, but tonight only the brighter side ought to be shown. "He might. You can't tell. Someday he might come riding across that bridge out there and—"

"And we'll be together again," Lucas finished. Tyler nodded as if that were so. What he didn't describe was the hard new look in Papa's eyes, how hollowed out his cheeks had become, that Ransom had fallen somewhere in the war. Even though Mama didn't weep easily, such details might make her cry, and her tears would frighten both Rosa Lee and Lucas.

Tyler finished his story by telling them what he believed was possible some far-off day. "A long time from now, maybe General Shelby will decide to come home again, not to carry on his grudge against the Union. Everyone who rode after him might follow him back just as quick. Can't tell; that might be the way it turns out." He wanted to believe the story himself. At Eagle Pass he'd decided to turn loose of his dream, but deep down, Tyler wondered if he ever could.

Then he told them about the old woman and her husband who'd lost their sons, Dolph and Joshua. He told them about Isaac, and showed off the pale scar on his

126

brow where Isaac's rock had nearly killed him. He told about the rainstorm in Texas when he'd run for high ground, about eating cactus (both Lucas and Rosa Lee wrinkled up their noses and made ugh sounds), about roasting lizards over a fire (hearing that, Rosa Lee jumped off her chair and said she'd never *ever* leave home if it meant you had to eat lizards).

But what could he tell them about Bigger?

How could he explain the first night Bigger slept by the fire? How mistrustful the dog had been, but how he'd finally made up? How to explain Bigger's strange eyes, his hard life of being poked and prodded until he turned into a devil? How he'd gotten free of the chain at Uncle Matt's, had followed along till he finally made friends? At least Mama and Lucas had a picture in their minds of Papa but how could he give them a picture of Bigger that would do the dog justice? Rather than tell something that would come out wrong, Tyler decided to say nothing at all.

After the potatoes had been put down in the root cellar in September, one evening when everyone was about to get ready for bed, Tyler announced he was going for a walk. Rosa Lee rubbed her eyes and wanted only to be tucked in with a story, but Lucas offered to tag along.

Together, under a few early stars and a quarter moon that hung low in the west, they walked across the bridge and went to visit Bigger's grave. In the falling dark of early autumn, Tyler could see by faint moonlight that tiny new green shoots were already rising from the black, loamy soil where Bigger lay sleeping.

Tyler told Lucas about the first time he'd laid eyes on Bigger. Soon he'd told him almost everything. (Talking

127

about Bigger was easier than talking about Papa.) "He was just about the best dog a person could have," he finished as he and Lucas sat side by side beneath the sister trees.

"Best how?" Lucas wanted to know.

Tyler tried to put his finger on it. "That man who beat on Bigger so bad was what folks call a scalawag," Tyler explained. "He robbed people and sold their stuff for money. It was Bigger's job to guard that man's wagon—but what he wanted, mainly, was just to be somebody's friend, to be a regular dog, not some monster people would call a devil."

"Too bad Mama gave all Maggie's pups away while you were gone," Lucas said, moving closer to Tyler in the dark. "You could a taken one of 'em, Ty. Maybe then you wouldn't miss Bigger so much." Suddenly Lucas's eyes got shiny in the silver light. "Why, you could a named your new dog Bigger too!"

Tyler felt the warmth of his brother's shoulder against his own. He shook his head, and looked down the slope, pale in the moonlight, down to the road, across the bridge that spanned Sweet Creek.

"No, Lucas," he said with a sigh, "because sometimes there's only one of a thing and nothing else can take its place. Whatever comes after has to be its own thing but can't ever be what you lost." Just like no matter how kind and good Uncle Matt was, he couldn't take Papa's place. The only person who could do that would be Papa himself.

Just the same, it was nature's way to make the best of things, Tyler realized, smoothing the new, fine-as-baby-hair grass with his fingertips. To make new beginnings and fresh starts; yes, that was nature's way.

Walking up the road with Lucas at his side, it came to Tyler how he might be able to do such a thing himself. It wouldn't bring Papa back—certainly not Bigger—nothing could do that. He laid an arm across his brother's shoulder. "In the morning I'm going down to Uncle Matt's," he told Lucas. "I owe him some money, and I want to tell him about Papa." He didn't tell Lucas what else he hoped to do while he was in New Hope.

Lucas reached up in the dark for Tyler's hand. "You're goin' to come back, though, ain't you, Ty?"

"Why, Lucas, you couldn't drive me off with a stick," Tyler replied. "Of course I'll come back. This is as fine a home place as a man could ever pick." Dear words; Papa's words.

This time Tyler arrived in New Hope just before the store closed. Uncle Matt was refolding a bolt of yard goods he'd been showing to a lady, and looked up with astonishment when he saw who was his last customer of the day.

"Why, Tyler!" he exclaimed. Then, a knowing look appeared in his eyes. Tyler was grateful some things didn't have to be explained to Uncle Matt. Somehow, he just *knew*. It saved a person the pain of trying to put into words what couldn't be contained so tidily.

"Ah, so that's how it turned out," Uncle Matt said simply. "Not all the casualties of war are on the battlefield, eh?" He smoothed the fabric and returned it to its place on a high shelf. He turned then, and rather than looking gloomy, seemed pleased at what he saw.

"But *you*, Tyler—look at you! Why, I think you've growed a whole inch while you were gone. As nephews

129

go, I'd say I got the pick of the litter," he declared, his eyes mild and smiling behind his glasses.

"That's what I wanted to talk to you about, Uncle Matt," Tyler answered.

"You want to talk about nephews?" Uncle Matt repeated, adjusting his spectacles, a puzzled frown carving furrows in his pale forehead.

"No, about litters."

"Litters?"

"Your little hound, that Daisy-dog you thought so much of, did she ever have those pups she got put in the family way with?"

A disgusted look came into Uncle Matt's eyes. "You might say so," he said peevishly. "Six of the little rascals came before she was all done. Last one was a runt that died straightaway. Other five were a motley collection, not a fine hound pup among 'em."

"Were?" Tyler questioned closely. "Did you drown 'em, then?" If Uncle Matt had been determined to shoot Bigger, it was entirely reasonable to suppose he'd get rid of Daisy's bastard pups.

"Oh, no, I didn't drown the misbegotten little wretches," Uncle Matt said, looking embarrassed. "It's not that I'm softhearted, mind you, but those pups were dear to Daisy—they were her young'uns, you see—it would a been a frustration to her if I'd stolen 'em away. She had 'em during the night, had 'em licked clean and took to nursing 'em right away. Maybe I should've drowned 'em in a water bucket but—"

"So you've still got 'em?"

"Only two, thank heavens!" Uncle Matt exclaimed.

"Folks from hereabouts took the others. There's a female left and one male—an ugly little devil if ever I saw one."

A devil if ever I saw one. . . .

"Can I see 'em?" Tyler asked.

"Best you come on in to supper now," Uncle Matt urged. "Clayton will be glad to see you, and later, if you still have a mind to, we can—"

"I'd rather see 'em now," Tyler said, not especially eager to see Clayton any quicker than he had to.

The pups were in the livery stable, enclosed in a chicken-wire pen made especially for them. "Me and Henry fixed this up on account of I can't let 'em run loose," Uncle Matt explained. "They're a wild pair, into everything—chasing chickens or horses or anything else that moves. Even stole Aunt Margaret's unmentionables off the clothesline one morning and dragged 'em all over town."

Uncle Matt grabbed the female pup by the loose skin of her neck, and held her out to Tyler. "She's a good girl," he admitted grudgingly, "for a mongrel, that is." The pup looked a lot like Daisy, Tyler saw, except that her speckled coat wasn't smooth but was dense, like a bear cub's might be. She thrashed energetically in his arms, finally twisting around so she could cover his face with a warm, wet tongue.

In the pen the male dog sat in three-quarter profile to greet his visitors. He was not as dark as Bigger, had a coat that was chestnut-hued rather than charcoal, had a bib pinned across his chest that was as white as if it'd been laundered only hours ago. When he turned full face, Tyler saw that he had one cool blue eye and one warm brown eye. Tyler set the wriggling female pup back in the pen beside her brother.

"If you're agreeable, Uncle Matt, I'll take that one off your hands," Tyler said quietly.

"But he's such a weird-looking critter with those queery eyes," Uncle Matt objected. "Why don't you take little Baby Daisy here?" he urged. "Him, why, nobody wants *him*. It's those spooky eyes that put folks off. You're the first one to show any interest in 'im a tall."

I would've made this trip sooner if I'd known you were here, Tyler thought, as he studied the pup.

Sooner. Yes, I surely would've come to New Hope sooner, he told the dog silently.

"No, he's the one I want. There's something about him," Tyler explained, without explaining that the most important thing was that he was Bigger's son, "and I don't mind his queer eyes. I mean, they're not his fault, are they? God gave 'em to him, right?"

Uncle Matt shrugged. "Appears to me you've got your mind made up, Tyler. Well, if he's your pick, he's the one you can have." Uncle Matt gave Tyler's shoulder a comforting squeeze.

That touch, so longed for from Papa, didn't feel the same from anyone else. Then Tyler remembered what he'd told Lucas: Everything has to find its own place. He turned, and gave Uncle Matt a hug as fleeting as the kiss he'd planted once on Lucas's brow. Uncle Matt would never be a man with a gypsy heart but he could be who he was; maybe that was enough.

"You always been downright good to me," Tyler mumbled against his uncle's storekeeper's smock.

"Why shouldn't I be?" Uncle Matt joshed, flustered

and pink with pleasure. "Aren't you my own sister's boy? The pick of the litter, too, as far as nephews go!"

Upstairs, as Tyler lay on the pallet Aunt Margaret had made up for him, Cousin Clayton once again thrashed around in his bedcovers. Finally he called across the darkness between them. "That dog ever follow after you, Cousin Tyler?"

The question surprised Tyler so much his eyes flew wide open. "What dog?" Clayton was a sly one; maybe it was best to feign stupidity.

"You know—that one my daddy had on a chain out there in the yard when you were here last time. The one he was fixin' to shoot."

"Oh. That one." Best, perhaps, to still pretend ignorance. Clayton was probably up to no good, as usual. "Oh. Yeah. Only for a little ways, though. Then I ran him off by pegging stones at 'im."

"You ever wonder how come he got loose, Cousin Ty?"

Tyler had imagined that somehow Bigger pulled himself out of his collar, even though he'd plainly seen by the worn-off hair around the dog's neck that he'd been tied tight. "Not much," he said, growing more curious about what Clayton had on his mind.

"I figured long as you was going so far off he might as well go with you," Clayton blurted. "Wasn't doing himself no good here! Papa aimed to have Henry take him out to the woods and get rid of him for sure. So after you left that day I got Henry to loosen his collar enough so's he could wiggle out of it." Clayton hesitated. Tyler was too startled to speak.

"I was . . ." Clayton hesitated again, and Tyler heard

133

the bedcovers being adjusted for the dozenth time. "I was scared to do it myself," Clayton confessed. "You got to admit, Cousin Ty, he *was* a mean-looking critter."

Tyler blinked several times in the dark. Why, you could never tell about a person, could you? Spoiled-rotten, Mama's-darling-brown-eyed-baby-boy Clayton had been worried enough about what might happen to Bigger (though of course he didn't know yet the dog's name was Bigger) that he'd asked Henry to help turn him loose.

"Say, Clayton. Would you like to come up and stay a while at Sweet Creek sometime?" Tyler asked, feeling suddenly generous.

"Stay . . . at . . . Sweet Creek?" Clayton repeated the words slowly, as if he marveled at the magic they might hold.

"Sure," Tyler went on. "You could get to know Lucas and Rosa Lee better. I'm not the only cousin you got, y'know. Fishing is good up there, too." He might even show Clayton where Bigger was buried. "There's lots to do, and if you don't mind sleeping on the floor like I'm doing now—"

"Why, it's mighty nice of you to ask," Clayton said, his voice round with wonder as he pictured what such a visit would be like. "But I never been away from home before, Cousin Ty," he complained, as if Sweet Creek were as far away as the Rio Grande. "Maybe my mama won't let—"

"Clayton, there's times when you have to do what you have to do," Tyler broke in.

Clayton was silent. "I guess you know all about that," he said at last. "Maybe I do, too. Not as much as you, but a little. I mean, ain't I the one who talked Henry into loosening up that dog's collar so he wouldn't get shot?"

134

"You did, for sure," Tyler agreed. Later, he would tell Clayton it hadn't kept Bigger from getting killed, but that was a story that could wait.

Tyler imagined Sooner curled in the straw of his chicken-wire pen out there in the livery barn, his strange eyes closed in sleep. Tomorrow they'd start home together. When spring came Clayton could come to spend a few days away from his mama for the first time in his whole life. They'd all go to visit Bigger's grave, even Rosa Lee if she wanted to, though Sooner—being a dog—wouldn't understand what it was all about and would only run around to pee on the three sister trees to leave his mark.

And someday—well, someday maybe Papa would come home. He might; how could a person say such a thing would never happen? Until then, Tyler vowed, he'd help Mama raise up Lucas and Rosa Lee. He'd go squirrel hunting with Sooner, and would teach Lucas how to hunt, too. Now it would be Sooner who'd lie on the hearth with Maggie.

Tyler studied the blocks of moonlight scattered on the floor of Clayton's bedroom. He'd lain here nearly five months ago, watching similar silver blocks. This time he thought of Isaac, and hoped the shoes had been a blessing. He thought of the blue-white aggie, safe in Papa's pocket. He thought of Bigger, sleeping for all time near the bridge that crossed Sweet Creek. His own journey was over; he'd come full circle. Now, there was the rest of life to be lived.

. . . AND AFTER

Tyler Bohannon was right about General Shelby.

In June 1867 the general recrossed the Rio Grande; many of his followers returned with him. They took advantage of the amnesty offered by President Andrew Johnson. Soon after, Joseph O. Shelby returned to his life as a farmer and manufacturer of rope in Bates County, Missouri. He invested in coal mining at Clarksville, and became associated with two small railroad companies in Saint Louis that would link the midwest to the whole nation. A fifth son was born to him in 1871, and his only daughter in 1875.

General Shelby was appointed to the post of United States Marshall in 1893, and Governor Thomas C. Fletcher reported that Shelby "worked night and day to restore peace by appealing to the people of Missouri to accept the new order of things." The general was proud to say he worked as hard for the Stars and Stripes as he'd once worked for the Stars and Bars. He died at Adrian, Missouri, on February 13, 1897, at the age of sixty-seven.

However, some members of the ragtag army of the

Lost Cause never set foot on United States soil again. A few men went to Canada, to Cuba, to as far away as England. Several remained in Mexico; some drifted deeper into Central America, ultimately even farther south, into Brazil and Venezuela. Perhaps such men continued to cherish the dream of someday restoring the Confederacy to its former glory.

The sons and daughters of those vanished men grew up, most married, had sons and daughters of their own. It became the job of everyone to rebuild a nation that had been divided by a war that left more than six hundred thousand men dead on battlefields with now-famous names like Gettysburg, Chickamauga, Manassas, and not-so-famous ones like Pea Ridge, Wilson's Creek, and Stones River.